Dennis Humphreys, now retired, lives in a Victorian house with a large garden in South Devon. In his professional career, he was a lawyer specialising in planning law. He has always been an active musician, playing keyboards and the flute. He has a wide range of interests, including Astronomy, English and French literature and history.

He has always been fascinated by the age of King Arthur, the time of the Anglo-Saxon invasions of Britain and of the migration of Britons to Brittany. Dennis has made a detailed study of the early period of Christianity, and of the development and status of the Church in the later Roman Empire.

To my history teacher at Christ College Brecon, Mr Bryan Richards, who sadly passed away recently, for giving me real enthusiasm for history, which I have retained ever since that time.

To Lord Melvyn Bragg for *'In Our Time'* on Radio 4 covering such a wide range of subjects in depth.

Dennis Humphreys

THE MIGRANTS

Britain and Brittany in the Fifth Century

AUSTIN MACAULEY PUBLISHERS®

LONDON • CAMBRIDGE • NEW YORK • SHARJAH

A CIP catalogue record for this title is available from the British Library.

ISBN 9781035869824 (Paperback)
ISBN 9781035869831 (ePub e-book)

www.austinmacauley.com

First Published 2025
Austin Macauley Publishers Ltd®
1 Canada Square
Canary Wharf
London
E14 5AA

To my dear wife, Liz, who passed away recently, for her help and support in my writing career, especially during lockdown.

To Sam, for reading my manuscript and sharing his thoughts with me.

Table of Contents

Preface
Holiday in Brittany

The sky was blue in Brittany that day in 2023, broken only by a few small white clouds. The sky was a pale blue, typical in Brittany, paler than the blue skies in Great Britain, even those in the far southwest. There was a sense of timelessness in this region of France with its own unique history, including its historic links with Celtic Britain from Roman times and even earlier. Breton, a Celtic language, was still spoken in the region and was part of its distinct character and heritage. The rocky shore line with small coves and hidden sandy beaches was reminiscent of Cornwall, but at the same time strangely different. There was a feeling that day that something was about to happen.

A recently retired British couple were spending a leisurely summer in their holiday cottage near the Breton town of Pont Aven. They were old friends of mine, whom I had met whilst we were at Cambridge. Bronwen Williams had read Celtic, Norse and Anglo-Saxon studies at Clare College and her boyfriend, Steve Rathbone, had read law at Sidney Sussex. Bronwen came away with starred first class honours and eventually became Professor of Celtic Studies at the University of Cardiff, and an authority on early Welsh history. She married Steve soon after leaving Cambridge and he pursued a successful career in the law. We kept in touch over the years and spent some very pleasant days with them in the cottage a few years back.

They had bought the grey stone cottage in a dilapidated condition many years earlier, and had gradually restored it to make it a comfortable place to stay and relax in that scenic part of France. It had a small fenced garden lovingly planted with hawthorn, rose bushes and fruit trees. They had chosen plants which could be left on their own for much of the year not needing attention from a gardener. The wisteria on the front of the cottage was now well established and admired by passers-by.

A local man, M. Keroch, kept an eye on the cottage, including its garden, and tended to the hedges and lawn, when the couple were absent. He was old enough to remember when it had been a fisherman's cottage in the distant past. With changes in commercial fishing since the war, the cottage had changed hands a few times, and the latest French owners had abandoned it for years having relocated to Paris to further their careers. Eventually, they had decided to sell, and the house then came into the hands of Steve and Bronwen. M. Keroch, a man who would never have dreamt of leaving this part of Brittany, was more than pleased to see how well the British couple had restored the cottage. Added to this was the fact that they blended in with the local way of life and spoke good French and even Breton at times.

Steve and Bronwen had spent most summer holidays there with their children. By this time, the children had grown up and left home. The kids sometimes used the cottage when their parents were not there, but usually went much further afield for their holidays. Bronwen and Steve were content now on their own in their much-loved cottage, and were looking forward to continuing with their relaxing vacation. They enjoyed the fine and sunny weather that day, and were pleased that the forecast was favourable: the weather was ideal for walks in the country or a dip in the sea or a day in historic Quimper or in maritime Concarneau.

They were both Francophiles and loved the culture and way of life in France and especially in Brittany. The fact that Bronwen was fluent in French sometimes caught out surly waiters, who were being rude about the English in her hearing. A similar thing happened a few years ago when a barman was acutely embarrassed when he found out that Bronwen was fluent in Breton.

This happened in a pub-type bar in the far north of Brittany, where the clientele were proud Bretons. The whole place was decked out in a Celtic/Breton style and may have been some sort of enclave for Breton nationalism. Bronwen and Steve wondered whether to go in there at all. Bronwen was not known for timidity and they boldly entered to hear the barman in a loud voice making disparaging remarks in Breton about the French and it seemed about everyone else who was not Breton. He was duly shocked when the newly arrived customer, a mature lady, who was clearly not a local, addressed him in fluent Breton.

Bronwen just said to him in his own language that, although she was Welsh and therefore a fellow Celt, she had many good friends in France (including Brittany) and in England. The barman was amazed that she had understood his remarks and had responded to him in a way which was mildly critical but also polite. He gave Bronwen and Steve a broad smile and drinks on the house. He was delighted to chat to her in Breton. He was not as bad as he had first seemed. He may just have been role-playing for the benefit of his customers and perhaps to boost trade.

Steve and Bronwen had been retired for a couple of years. Like others in the same time of life and with some financial resources, they had big plans for their remaining years of active life, such as a visit to Steve's brother and family in New Zealand, a safari trip to Tanzania, the Inca sites in Peru, Angkor Wat in Cambodia, and many more. For the past few years they had contented themselves with Brittany, but were becoming enthusiastic about trips further afield. They were reasonably well-off for money, but their ambitious plans were expensive and careful planning and assessment of priorities would be needed.

But one day during their current holiday, having had a discussion about visits to far off places, Bronwen and Steve were enjoying a good strong expresso coffee at a pavement café in Pont Aven and watching the world go by. Their period of relaxation was suddenly broken by a thunderbolt. There was a news report in their copy of the regional newspaper, Ouest-France, that an ancient manuscript had been discovered at the former Abbey of Ponterle[1], written in the early Brythonic language, the tongue spoken in Britain from ancient times, during the Roman period and thereafter. It was the predecessor of modern Welsh, Cornish and Breton. Bronwen was amazed and excited by this report and kept reading and rereading it. It was the stuff of dreams for her.

This old abbey had not been used for ecclesiastical purposes since the upheaval of the French Revolution. Almost all its original buildings had gone and there had been much rebuilding and alterations in the Middle Ages and in later years. A twelfth-century chapel and a simple and elegant main building survived with little subsequent alteration. The old abbey was still a magnificent and much loved-sight in the rural Breton landscape. It was a living reminder of times gone by. Local people felt that these buildings were part of a long and unbroken tradition. Although Brittany like the rest of France was generally secular in outlook, the ancient surviving Christian buildings still gave an indelible sense of identity to many people.

Over the years, the abbey had been used for a variety of purposes, including education, and was currently occupied by an international charitable organisation

---

[1] A fictional place

which provided a place of retreat and meditation. This organisation was well-funded and was in the course of carrying out some building works. During a deep excavation to put in a new sewer, a battered and rusty metal trunk was found containing a number of ancient manuscripts, including the one in the Brythonic language. This was wedged between a beautifully illustrated manuscript copy of the Latin Vulgate Bible (a wonderful find in itself) and an early copy in Latin of the *City of God*, by the great Catholic theologian, St Augustine of Hippo.

Fortunately, the local builder, Gaston, who discovered the trunk, had previous experience of excavations at historic sites. He had also been unable to use excavators in the immediate vicinity of the ancient chapel, where the trunk was found and where he and his workers had to resort to hand tools to finish the excavation. And so the trunk emerged unscathed. The builder was as excited as anybody at the discovery and was keen to know whether the trunk contained anything of value. He was thinking of gold coins hidden away during the French Revolution. But he was more than pleased to learn that it contained ancient manuscripts. Specialist archaeologists were rushed to the scene from Quimper. The trunk was carefully opened in situ by an archaeologist in the presence of the builders, the site owners and several onlookers. There were gasps of excitement when the manuscripts were found inside. They were fragile and were handled with great care by the archaeologists. At the time no one knew quite what they were, although it was obvious that they were very old.

The documents were immediately passed over to the University of Nantes, where they were carefully preserved and examined. In some cases, they had to be pieced together. It was discovered that the manuscript in early Brythonic (also known as Common Brittonic) contained a poem with the romantic title of 'The Song of Cadwur'. As a result of scientific tests and expert study of the language used, this document itself was estimated to be from the twelfth-century CE, but the consensus view of scholars was that it was, in fact, a copy of an original document from an earlier century containing an even older poem, which told of events in the fifth century. There was no evidence as to its author, and the speculation was that the poem was a seventh century written version of an older oral poem, composed either in Brittany or in Great Britain, probably in the fifth century.

Bronwen knew the academics at Nantes who specialised in Celtic Studies and, with great excitement, asked if she could come and see the document. This was readily agreed, as she was a well-known authority on this ancient language and on the history of that period in Britain and in Brittany. She had written several authoritative textbooks on these subjects and was a regular speaker at lectures and seminars on that period, in the UK, France and the USA.

The fifth century had always fascinated her, being a time of such rapid and momentous change in Britain and continental Europe, but with little or no contemporary written records regarding events in Britain and indeed in Brittany. It was also the age of the mythical King Arthur, about whom Bronwen had written a popular and successful book. She was keen to study the newly discovered document, not just for its artistic merit, but also for the insight it might give as to the history of this darkest part of the so-called Dark Ages, which fascinated her. She was able to confirm the opinion of the academics at the university as to the age of the document, i.e., that it was a copy of an original seventh century manuscript and that the oral poem itself had probably been composed in the fifth century. From her studies over a long period, she was aware of how the Brythonic language had evolved over the centuries and this knowledge enabled her to give her expert opinion about the document.

Any idea of a normal relaxing holiday was over. The University of Nantes, a very busy teaching and research institution, was more than pleased to second Bronwen to work on the Brythonic manuscript. She visited Nantes many times and eventually ended up staying with Steve in the cottage near Pont Aven rather longer than previously intended. Steve wanted to go back to Wales but stayed with Bronwen. He took the opportunity to play some golf (a game which he found frustrating), and do some sea-angling, (occasionally catching a fish). He was the sort of person who was very good at one thing (being a lawyer), but not much good at anything else.

The exception was baking: he had spent much time over the years watching cookery programmes on TV and thereby picked up some ideas. His Far Breton was excellent and his crêpes and galettes were much admired. He cooked in the style of a lawyer. He always needed a recipe, which he expected to be full, clear and precise. When the recipe specified 'two eggs', for, example, he thought it should have specified 'large, medium or small'. He would always follow the recipe precisely. Steve was a friendly and sociable character and people found him good company.

Under the post-Brexit rules, they had to go back to the UK after a few weeks anyway. Bronwen thought of applying for a work visa allowing her to remain longer but could not be bothered with all the red tape. She had always disliked bureaucracy of any kind and even in her university days she had at times fallen out with admin staff and their tedious forms.

In the next months in their bungalow at Dinas Powys, Bronwen was in her element, spending her days in intensive study of a very accurate photocopy of the document, including trying to work out what it had said in those few parts which were missing. The general drift of the story was very clear to her. After many hours of work (a true labour of love for her), Bronwen had translated this long poem into modern Welsh, into English and into French—all prose translations. In the following year, the Poet Laureate, Sir Stephen Armstrong, who much admired the ancient story, composed an excellent version in verse of Bronwen's English translation. Professor Dilwyn ap Hywel of Bangor University wrote a brilliant modern Welsh version of the poem. This was later recited in full at the National Eisteddfod.

Even when her academic studies and translations had been completed, Bronwen just could not get the story out of her head. It was like one of those tunes which kept coming back to you and which you could not shake off. There was a term for that phenomenon but she could not remember what it was. She decided to write a novel in Welsh based on the characters and events in the poem, allowing herself a large amount of artistic licence. As a historian writing the novel, much of it was based on history or as much of history as was known. All the events in the manuscript were included plus many purely fictional elements. She tried hard to ensure that these fictional elements were in tune with how life might have been at that time, and that any anachronisms were studiously avoided. She aimed to bring that period of history back to life and in a way as relevant as possible to the modern reader.

Over this long period, Steve saw little of her, as she was closeted away in her study for hours on end. Sometimes she would work into the small hours and wake Steve up when she was finally getting into bed. The whole process was so exciting for her, including the fact that the document contained the earliest reference to 'Arthur'.

Her novel, entitled 'The Song of Cadwur' in her English translation, now follows.

The Song of Cadwur
A Novel by Bronwen Williams

Chapter 1
A Letter from Armorica[2]

In the Year of our Lord 460, in the town of Trepunek[3] in the part of north-west Armorica known as Domnonia[4], Owain, a landowning farmer of substantial means, was preparing to write an important letter to his brother in Britannia. Owain was one of nature's optimists, usually with a smile on his face, which was round and enhanced with rosy cheeks. This letter was something he had been contemplating for several days and now he had made his mind up to get down to business and write it. It was rare for him (or most other people) to write letters in those days, and the importance of this one, added to his lack of practice, caused him to feel anxious. He was wealthy enough to be able to afford to employ a scribe, but felt confident that he could write the letter himself. He had all the materials necessary to do so.

Owain was bilingual, in the British language (Common Brittonic) and in Latin, and, like many of the wealthier people of or from Britannia at the time, fluent in both. He could also converse with some difficulty in the dialect of the old Gaulish tongue as spoken by some of the older generation in the eastern part of Armorica. When he wrote anything, he normally did so in Latin, as he found it easier to spell Latin words than their equivalent in the British tongue, which was mainly a spoken language.

And so, using Latin, he composed the letter with great care and much thought:

---

[2] Armorica was the Latin name for what is now Brittany and adjoining territory

[3] A fictional town

[4] This is the name of part of Armorica, named after Dumnonia, the Roman name for Devon (sometimes including Cornwall)

To my beloved and devout brother, Teged, cordial greetings from the town of Trepunek in Armorica.

I sincerely hope that this letter will find you, Sioned, and your dear children in good health.

I am deeply distressed to learn that, according to all reports, times are hard and unpredictable in Britannia[5], with ever more pagan Saxons invading the island, and with continuing damaging raids by the ungodly Scoti[6] and Picti[7]. Even as far west as our ancient and well defended land of Powys, I am told you face the risk of Saxon incursions, after the so-called Saxon revolt.

Life is so different, dear Brother, here in Armorica. We and many of our fellow countrymen have found tranquillity and prosperity in this fine region, one of the most peaceful parts of Gaul. We enjoy good relations with other British residents here, many of whom migrated to this region years ago.

We have always received a warm welcome from the few Gaulish folk living in Armorica, devout god-fearing people who know of the love of our Saviour, the Lord Jesus Christ. This is a very large region with few people, so there is no shortage of space for newcomers such as ourselves.

In this favoured land with its temperate climate, its rich and fertile soils produce a wide range of cereal crops, as well as fruits and vegetables. There is also much fine pasture land for our cattle, sheep and draught horses.

There are many springs with pure fresh waters. Our rivers are not scenic like the Hafren[8], but in some stretches their pure waters are home to some fine trout, plentiful eels and the occasional salmon. Shellfish of all kinds abound on our shores and our seas are rich in fish.

I know dear Brother how you love hunting. Well, our forests and moors are full of game: deer, wild boar, hares, pheasants and other fowl.

We have a simple church in the town, where on each Lord's Day we celebrate the Eucharist as administered by our Deacon Emyr, a devout man of simple and ascetic life-style, devoted to works of charity.

I urge you and your family, dear Brother, to come to Armorica and join us here. I could certainly use your help on the farm as I am beginning to feel my age, with rheumatic pains at times.

---

[5] The Latin name for what is now England and Wales, more or less

[6] The name given to invaders from the north of Ireland

[7] Inhabitants of what is now Scotland, mainly from the Highland.

[8] The British/Welsh name for the River Severn. Its Latin name was Sabrina

I am sure that you would have a better life here, and your children would have a better future than in Britannia, a land dominated and threatened by ignorant pagan Saxons and ravaged by the murderous Scoti and Picti. There is a newly established monastic foundation not far away, offering education to boys in Latin, theology and rhetoric.

There are frequent sailings of stout merchant ships from the British ports in Cornubia[9] and Dumnonia[10] to our many ports. Most of them offer passage to travellers. I am told that the passage of goods and people between southwest Britannia and Armorica has been going on for centuries, even long before the Romans arrived in Gaul. The rich minerals in Cornubia must have been a magnet for this trade.

I sincerely hope that you will decide to join us in Armorica, where you will receive a warm welcome from me and Gwen, and from our children, who would love to see their cousins. Likewise a warm welcome from our whole community.

I pray every night for your health and your safety in these troubled times, and now, dear Brother, send you all my love.

Owain ap Geraint.

He read his letter over again to check the spelling and grammar, as best he could. It was many years since he was taught Latin by a Roman scholar at Deva[11]. He knew that his was not now the Latin of Cicero and Virgil, but people understood his Latin and he was content that his brother would do so. He too had been taught by the same scholar.

When he had finished the letter, he realised how emotional he felt, partly from his love for his brother but mainly because it brought to mind his father, Geraint, who sadly had died from a plague whilst Owain was still living in Britannia. His father was often known by the Roman version of his name, Gerontius. Owain's mother had died a few years earlier. It was only after the death of both parents that Owain could contemplate emigration to Armorica.

He remembered what a wonderful childhood he and Teged had enjoyed under their father's care. He had taught them almost everything they knew: how to ride, to hunt, to till the land, to tend to farm animals, and to use weapons of

---

[9] The Roman name for Cornwall

[10] The Roman name for Devon

[11] The Roman name for Chester

war. Under Roman rule, the Britons (except for those who were in the Roman legions) were not trained in warfare, but with the withdrawal of the Roman legions from Britannia, many Britons had acquired weapons of war and had learnt to use them, sometimes with training from those Romano-British warriors who remained.

Things had also started to change in the final stages of Roman rule, as all the signs were that the Roman legions would be leaving before long, in view of the troubled condition of the Western Roman Empire. Britons realised that they would need to defend their country by themselves. The eventual withdrawal of all three legions was a massive loss to the Britons, and the defence of their country was a daunting challenge. All British freemen were Roman citizens by these times. This included Owain and his sons on reaching adulthood. His paternal grandmother, Lydia, was from a noble Roman family based in Gaul. This explains why Owain's father liked to use the name Gerontius at times, to remind others that he had Roman blood.

Thinking of his father, Owain had particular memories of long and happy summer days beside the Hafren, in the vicinity of Llanfair-yn-Nghedewain[12], where there were sandy banks and where the river water was deep and calm enough for swimming in its green waters. Most local people had not learnt to swim and could only bathe in the shallower water. Geraint was a good swimmer and taught both his sons how to swim, a pastime they much enjoyed on long summer days, particularly after all the hard work of gathering in the harvest. Owain remembered the shock on entering into the cold water on a hot day and then the burst of energy it gave him as he swam along with powerful strokes. After the swim he would lie on the riverbank under the weeping willows and gradually dry off in company with his father and brother. He could still even now remember the smell and taste of the river and the gently abrasive sensation of the long grass on the riverbank as they rested upon it after the swim.

Owain thought he could have added more to the letter about the wild life in Domnonia: the carpets of harebells in the nearby woods in spring time hosting their hares with their unbridled antics; and the blankets of cowslips in the meadows. At night, the howls of wolf packs could be heard along with the hooting of owls.

Owain also recalled vividly how difficult the decision to leave Britannia had been. He loved his homeland dearly and was closely attached to it. He also had

---

[12] Welsh name for the place now called Newtown Powys.

a well-established farm and other assets there, which he would need to leave behind. He had many friends, including the members of the congregation in his local church. Most of all he would miss Teged, his brother, who had decided to remain in Britannia as long as he possibly could. He was an active member of a militia and was prepared to fight against any invaders to protect his homeland. He also had a prosperous business as a horse-breeder and trader. His ties to Britannia were therefore rather stronger than those of Owain. So 'some years previously the brothers had said a tearful farewell, as Owain was departing for a new life over the seas. He recalled how distraught Gwen had been on saying farewell to her family.

With these recollections and thoughts in his mind, Owain travelled on the following day to the busy port of Tregaran[13] on the north coast of Domnonia. Tregaran was a place which he loved. It reminded him of similar ports on the west coast of Cambria, which he had regularly visited with his family in his boyhood. That day there were all sorts of boats bobbing on the sea in or around Tregaran harbour: sea-going galleons of noble Roman appearance, smaller sailing ships for travel along the coasts of Armorica, and numerous fishing boats, from small day boats with a crew of two to larger trawlers to fish in deeper waters. There always seemed to be much bustle and activity in the harbour area and in the town square: fishermen and their wives repairing nets, boats being cleaned and varnished, and from the market the shouts of the traders to attract the customers to their goods. There were often musicians playing and singing and sometimes joined by folk dancers.

Owain was pleased to see the Star of Bethlehem at its mooring. Captain Gwynfor waved to him and then came ashore in his tender. The two men talked for a while and then Owain entrusted his letter, suitably bound up and sealed to Captain Gwynfor, a ship's master who had sailed across those waters for over thirty years. The procedure for the delivery of letters and goods was well known to him: the captain would place the letter with his cousins in Dumnonia (the British kingdom). They were well practised in making deliveries to all parts of Britannia still under British control. The two men said their farewells and Owain then saw the fine sailing ship, which had been loaded with a valuable cargo of pottery, grain, oil, olives and wine, set sail for Isca, aided by a stiff breeze from the southwest. On its return journey, the cargo would probably be tin, copper, lead and sheep's wool and leather.

---

[13] A fictional town

Chapter 2
The Good Samaritan

On a cloudy afternoon, with a refreshing breeze, Owain, with his head still full of the sounds and smells of the port, began his journey back to Trepunek in his fine horse-drawn cart. At the market square he had bought some provisions, which he had covered up carefully, in case the rain might set in later in the day. He was pleased to find some oriental spices there, which were not often available at Trepunek, and which were much used in cooking at that time, especially by those familiar with Roman recipes. He also purchased olive oil and his favourite wine from southern Gaul in large terracotta jars. There were also jars of fine local honey for sale. He bought some to supplement the honey available at Trepunek. Having handed over the letter to the excellent sea captain, he felt he had done all he could to encourage his dear brother to come to Armorica. His accustomed smile again illuminated his affable face. It was now up to Teged to decide whether to remain in Britannia and continue in the resistance to the Saxons or to come to Armorica for a safer and better life. He could not tell which way Teged might decide.

The route home was well known to him, having made the journey many times over the years. It was one of the few good cart tracks in the area and linked the important port of Tregaran to the main Roman road to Condate[14]. He knew every steep gradient, the location of the worst potholes, and where to find an inn for refreshment for himself, his steward, Ifor, and of course, for the horse. There were many hazel trees along the route and in autumn it was a popular area for collecting nuts before the squirrels took them all. The weather remained dry and they were making good progress, when they both noticed something unexpected on the highway verge, in the midst of bracken and thick brambles.

---

[14] Rennes. Its full name in Latin was Condate Redonum

What they saw looked like a person in the foetal position lying on the verge. As they were not sure whether they were looking at a live person or a dead body or something else altogether, they stopped abruptly, tied the horse's halter to a stout tree, and walked back the few yards to the verge where the body lay, wondering what they would find. As they stood over the body, they realised it was a man of about thirty years of age, clutching two capacious bags close to his body. As they looked him over, he moved slightly and opened his tired and bloodshot eyes. He looked thin, pale and haunted, and obviously fearful of the two men who had come to see him.

Owain spoke to him in Brythonic but realised that the man did not understand a word of what he had said. It was clear that he was not from Armorica. Owain then spoke in Latin slowly and as clearly as he could (in anxious but kindly tones), "Are you ill or injured, sir, and can we help you? Please do not be afraid."

The man groaned, as if in some discomfort, but looked a little relieved, believing that he was not in danger from these two men. He seemed to have understood what Owain had said to him. Taking a deep breath, he replied in a dialect of Latin, which Owain could barely understand, "I had come from eastern Gaul near the banks of the great River Rhenus[15], with a group of men from our village. It had been attacked by a gang of blood-thirsty Alani[16], who took over our part of the village and drove us out. We journeyed west for several days, hoping to find sanctuary in Armorica. I got separated from the group when we were attacked by bandits near Condate Redonum. Some of us escaped, but we became separated. I have not seen any member of the group since, and have staggered on as far as here, but I am now exhausted."

Owain was very distressed to hear his story, but gave him one of his customary cordial smiles and asked, "Would you like to come with us, sir, to Trepunek, which is not too far away? We can give you somewhere to rest until you are recovered."

Rather surprised by this unexpected offer, the man responded, "That would be most welcome. It is the first kindness I have experienced on this long and difficult journey. If I stay here any longer I will surely die where I lie."

They helped him on the short walk back to the cart and to get on board. Owain offered to take his bags to assist him, but, although weak, he held on to them tightly. Apologetically, he explained, "These bags contain the only few

---

[15] The Rhine
[16] One of the tribes which invaded Gaul in the fifth century

possessions of my dear father, who died of apoplexy when we were attacked by the loathsome Alani."

Owain empathised with the man's feelings, given his own fond memories of his own father, and so left the bags with him. He gave him some water to drink and some bread and cold pork to eat. The man was obviously very thirsty and hungry, and expressed his gratitude.

Owain with a warm smile then said, "I am Owain and I farm some land at Trepunek. This is my steward and good friend, Ifor. What is your name, sir?"

"I have a Gaulish name which I was given at birth, but as from my teens I have used my Roman name, Claudius."

They travelled on, with Ifor taking the reins, and with Claudius half asleep in the cart. These events reminded Owain of the parable of the Good Samaritan. Without any pride or self-satisfaction, he felt he was acting according to God's will.

When they reached the town, Owain told his wife, Gwen, about their passenger. As ever a busy and active lady, she quickly made up a bed for him and gave him some venison stew to eat. Gwen was by her very nature a motherly person, and she sought to look after Claudius in a caring but unassuming way.

He said how grateful he was and then, exhausted, he went to rest on the bed.

Gwen was delighted with the items which her husband had brought from Tregaran.

Claudius stayed with them for a few days, but one morning they found his bed empty with no sign of him. He had left a note on the pillow on a wax tablet, written in rather poor Latin and barely legible, expressing his gratitude for their hospitality and kindness, adding that he had dreamt in the night that the remaining members of the group were nearby. He had decided to leave at dawn to try to find them. Owain and Gwen were surprised and a little anxious for him, but there was nothing they could do about it. Ifor, who had a more suspicious nature, was not particularly surprised and had not altogether trusted Claudius. Owain joked with him. "You are from Cornubia and therefore do not like any foreigners!"

Ifor never short of an answer responded, "Not so. We like to see what they are up to before we make up our minds about them."

After dispatching his important letter, Owain was continually thinking of his brother. He wondered how long it would take for the letter to reach him and when and how he would respond. He acknowledged that Teged had business interests at home as well as his role as a member of the militia.

Having these thoughts about his brother one day, Owain was sitting at the steps of his farmhouse. He recalled what the property had been like when they first moved in. It had been severely damaged after a terrible raid by pirates, who had slaughtered its male occupants and taken its women as slaves. Some barns and outbuildings had been burnt to the ground. But a number of byres and bothies remained undamaged. These pirates had been more intent on taking booty and slaves than wasting time in destroying buildings. The premises had been taken over by the local ruler, in the absence of anyone left to claim ownership, and was handed over to Owain soon after his arrival in Armorica.

As Owain now looked at his property, he felt proud of all the work which he and his household had carried out. The farmhouse had been restored. New barns had been built, along with a watermill, used to grind corn. This involved restoring the system of leats, which took water from the nearby River Punek to feed the mill wheel. He did not do the milling himself but had let the mill to Trefor, who milled grain there from Owain's farm and for other farmers in the vicinity. There was a fine vegetable and herb garden, a duck pond, and the arable fields and pastures. He had thought of putting in beehives, but had discarded the idea as bee-keeping was not one of his skills.

Owain particularly liked the line of birch trees along the driveway up to the farmhouse and the little orchard at the side of the house. He had planted both of these features himself. The orchard was a dual source for pleasure for him, with magical blossom in spring and hopefully a fine crop of fruit in the autumn. Gwen maintained colourful flower beds along the house frontage. The property was as close in character and appearance they could get to the house which they had left behind in Powys.

There was still some risk of piracy whether from Germanic or Hibernian[17] invaders, but security was much improved by the local ruler and his well-trained militia. Owain, his staff and servants all kept swords, spears and daggers and were well able to defend themselves from all but the most powerful invaders. It was, however, many years since there had been any problem with security in their town and district. It seemed that such invaders must have turned their attention to the fertile lands in the south and east of Britannia.

---

[17] Hibernia, meaning the land of winter, was the Roman name for Ireland

Chapter 3
A Day in the life of Emyr, the Deacon

Some days after the dispatch of the letter, on a Sunday morning, the Eucharist was being celebrated in the little local timber-built church of Trepunek administered by the Deacon Emyr. In the very early days of the Western Church, the liturgy had been in Greek, but now it was mainly in Latin, the vernacular language understood by most people of the Western Roman Empire. This was fortunate, as although Emyr could read, write and speak Latin, he was not educated in Greek. As this was a remote area, a deacon was allowed to administer the Eucharist if no cleric of higher rank was available. Although this was strictly speaking contrary to Papal regulations, it happened through necessity away from the larger cities and settlements. The church was once a grain store, but had been converted to its new use. An altar and baptistery had been installed.

The service began with a reading from the Book of Psalms in Latin by the deacon, followed by the Eucharist and the taking of the bread and wine. Then some simple hymns were sung in Latin accompanied by Celtic lyres. The deacon then read passages from the letters of St Paul and preached a short sermon on the subject of charity, with emphasis on helping those in need.

After the service, refreshments were taken in the nearby hall, and then the congregation made their way home. Deacon Emyr's work, however, had not yet been completed. He was aware of a remote cottage a few miles from the village, where the residents had been struck down by a fever. The family there, including their four young children, had little food. Emyr collected some basic foodstuffs, including donations from members of the congregation. He packed them into his two dark brown leather bags, and also included some communion bread and wine. He had use of a horse and was a competent rider, but, as was his custom, he chose to walk on this occasion.

In the late afternoon, feeling a little tired but keen to do his duty, he set off on the coast path towards the family's cottage. After about two miles, he sat down for a rest on a rocky bank overlooking the sea, with an old oak wood nearby. He saw the fine sight of a merchant ship in full sail heading towards some distant port, probably in the region of Naoned[18]. He thought how wonderful it was that men had used their God-given ingenuity to produce such a majestic vessel. Being now rather more tired from his day's exertions, he stretched out on a grassy patch and soon dropped off to sleep. When he awoke, he saw that dusk was just beginning to set in on an evening with a small crescent moon. He was annoyed with himself for being slothful and asked God's forgiveness. He regretted keeping the poor residents of the cottage waiting.

Whilst he was still entertaining these feelings and also contemplating the beauty of God's creation, he heard a noise behind him, but he took little notice, as he thought it must be a deer or other animal in the oak wood treading on leaves or fallen twigs. Suddenly he felt strong arms around his neck, and he was pushed onto his back so quickly that he had no time to think. For a split second, he saw two masked men standing over him and a long Spanish sword in the hands of one of them. He was immediately stabbed through the heart and left to die. As the men moved away, Emyr uttered a few words addressed to the Lord and then gave up his soul. It all happened so suddenly and so rapidly that it seemed he must have suffered little pain. A life had been extinguished in an instant. It was the precious life of a truly good man.

Shortly afterwards, the body of this pious man was found by two shepherds, who had been leading their flocks to pastures new. Knowing Emyr so well, they were utterly shocked at the sight of this much-loved man of the Church lying dead in a pool of blood. He still had near him his bags containing foodstuffs and his wallet. It seemed that nothing had been taken. His face was absolutely serene as if he was looking at a vision of Heaven. On his body, they saw a neat pile of acorns in a sort of circle rising up in a cone shape. They checked that he had no pulse and it was obvious that he was not breathing. His body was not yet really cold but it was certain that he was dead. They had dealt with enough animals to know the difference between the living and the dead.

In the semi-darkness, a cart was brought to carry his body back to the town, where it was laid in the church. The news spread fast. The whole town was filled with shock, horror and grief. *Who could possibly have committed such a vile and*

---

[18] Breton name for Nantes

wicked act and for what possible reason? It did not look like robbery as his bags, still full, were left a little way from his body and his wallet with money in it was not taken. He had no enemies and indeed he was loved by all who knew him. Crime of any sort in this part of Armorica at this time was virtually unheard of. *What was the significance of the acorns?* No one in the town could even guess what, if anything, they were meant to signify.

One of the shepherds was given a horse and he willingly took the food and provisions to the residents of the cottage. Although it was now getting quite dark, both he and the horse knew the way to this cottage. When there, he had the distressing task of telling the residents of the terrible event which had happened. They wept bitter tears but appreciated the foodstuff so generously donated to them. In the event, it went a long way to help with their gradual recovery to health. They would soon return to the church for the Eucharist.

Arrangements were made for the burial of Emyr in the cemetery, located on the boundary of the town. The burial ceremony was performed by Owain, as a senior member of the community, who spoke Latin well enough and was familiar with the words of the burial service, which he was able to read from a liturgical manuscript kept at the church. The burial had to be conducted in that way, as no member of the clergy would be able to get to the town for several days. It was a desperately sad event. Owain could not hold back his tears and there was much weeping and wailing by those present. Some felt that without their deacon, the community was isolated and would not have the protection of the Lord.

A messenger had been sent to Condate Redonum, to inform the bishop about this terrible tragedy and to ask for help in the investigation of the murder and also for the blessing of the deceased. The tragic loss of Emyr also meant that a replacement member of the clergy would be needed. The residents in deep shock and mourning, and with feelings of isolation and vulnerability, waited anxiously for a response from the bishop.

The noble ruler of this part of Armorica was informed of the tragic event by a messenger, and was as shocked as all others who had heard this news. He could offer no explanation but promised to make enquiries from members of the local militia, who might have some ideas about criminals or hostile groups in that area. Nothing whatsoever emerged from these enquiries. The fact that nothing was stolen ruled out the idea of involvement by pirates or highwaymen.

Chapter 4
The Four Horsemen

Four skilled and elegant horsemen were nearing the end of their journey from Condate Redonum to Trepunek. The group was led by a man with a fine bearing and posture, suggestive of a military background. There was a pronounced scar on the right side of his face. This was the only blemish on his handsome countenance. This fine rider was a presbyter of the Church, ordained originally by the famous Bishop of Autissiodorum[19], but now based at Condate, where there were a number of bishops and presbyters ministering to the folk of the city and its wide hinterland.

This leading horseman had been born in Britannia, the eldest son of a Roman centurion. His wider family had emigrated to Gaul after being driven from their land by the Saxons. When he had become an adult, he joined the Roman army in Gaul. He became part of the forces led by the Roman Consul and General Flavius Aëtius. His name was Joseph, a name which he had taken after his ordination. As a young soldier, he had fought as a proud member of the great allied army in the Year of our Lord 451, when in the fields of Catalaunia[20] that army had defeated that Devil incarnate, Attila, and his hoard of Huns, who then left Gaul for Italia. The great allied army led by Aëtius consisted of Romans, Gallo-Romans, Visigoths under their King Theodoric, Alemanni, Franks, a large militia from Armorica and others. This was the first time that the dreaded Huns had been decisively halted in their vile rampage against the western world. Soon afterwards, Attila himself was to die in Italia and the Huns would cease to terrorise the world. The battle scar on Joseph's face was the result of a blow from the enemy in that battle, which he was fortunate to survive.

---

[19] Auxerre
[20] This refers to the Battle of Châlons

On arrival at Trepunek, these horseman were given a warm welcome by Owain and Gwen, as well as by other residents of the town. It was a big event in the life of the tranquil town to receive four visitors such as these. Joseph, a man of presence and charisma, responded, "We are delighted to visit you at your fine town in this beautiful countryside, but regret that our visit should be in the aftermath of the foul murder committed here.

"May I introduce my companions? This is Daniel, who is a deacon of the Church, and whom the bishop has asked to serve your community. He has been authorised to conduct the Eucharist, when higher ranking clergy are not available as in the more remote parts of Armorica. Daniel is a young man of deep faith and he is very learned in the Holy Scriptures and the writings of our religious leaders, such as Bishop Augustine[21]."

Owain replied with a warm smile on his cheerful face, addressing his remarks to Daniel, "You are most welcome here, sir, and it will be a great comfort to our people to receive the Eucharist from a holy man appointed by our beloved bishop."

Daniel, obviously a serious young man, if a little austere, said, "I hope I will serve God and the congregation with the same charity and devotion as my much respected predecessor."

Joseph then introduced the other two colleagues, who were in their late teens, "This is Luke and this is Matthew. They are cousins, originally from Britannia, who currently work on their family's large estate near Condate. Luke is considering entering the monastic life at the abbey recently established at Ponterle in the south of Domnonia. I will be riding there with him after we have departed from Trepunek, to meet the abbot and to allow Luke to gain greater insight into the life of a monk. This will help him to decide on his future. Matthew was keen to join us on our journey, as he had not previously been in the more western parts of Armorica."

Gwen joined them and explained with her usual mixture of kindness, enthusiasm and efficiency, "I have prepared refreshments for you, gentlemen, if you would like to join me in the dining room."

Joseph, appreciating the warmth of her welcome, looked kindly at her and responded, "Thank you. That is most kind. But first I should like a few words in private with Owain, if I may. Daniel, Luke and Matthew, please proceed with

---

[21] This is the theologian from North Africa, who became St Augustine of Hippo, not to be confused with the later St Augustine of Canterbury

our generous hostess. Owain and I will remain here for a few moments to talk about poor Deacon Emyr, so that I may be made familiar with all the known facts about this tragic event."

The three guests left with Gwen, whilst Joseph and Owain remained in the hall.

Joseph began speaking in very sympathetic tones. "Do we know what exactly happened on that awful evening?"

"I am not sure that we do. But I can tell you all I know. Two shepherds found his body just after dark, in a pool of blood. They think it was about mid-way between six and seven hours of the evening. This was beside the coast path a few miles west of here. It is a well-known spot, with good views of the coast and the sea. He was on his way to a remote cottage to take food for a family who had been suffering from the fever. He was travelling alone on foot, as this is what he often did. It is normally perfectly safe for people to walk about alone in this area.

"He had been fatally stabbed, but nothing had been stolen. His purse was not taken and, although his bags were moved a few feet from him, they were left there untouched, still with the food in them, also the bread and communion wine.

"As the weather had been dry, I am told there was no sign of footprints, or of horses or vehicles being present. We don't know when the awful act was committed. We think he left here at about half past the hour of three and he was found at about half past the hour of six. He should easily have reached the cottage by then. It should have taken him no more than about an hour to get to where he was found, near the oak wood. It seems that he must have been killed not that long before half an hour past the sixth hour. The body was still slightly warm when the shepherds found him, but he had no pulse and was not breathing. They did not see anyone about the location.

"A strange thing was that they found a neat pile of acorns on his chest: near his heart."

Joseph carefully took in this information and looked both sad and perplexed. Owain felt quite distressed giving this account and had tears in his eyes. Joseph knew how Owain must have been feeling and paused for a moment before asking him any further questions. Then he continued, making his enquiries as sensitively as he could.

"Did Emyr have any enemies? Was there someone with a grudge against him?

"Did any suspicion fall on the shepherds?"

"Emyr was the most benevolent man in the world and was well loved by everyone who ever met him. The shepherds knew him well and were on very friendly terms with him. Whenever their work requirements allowed, they attended divine service with us."

"How much do we know of Emyr's past life?"

"He has lived here practically all his life. He came here with his parents years ago from Cornubia. He was married some years back but sadly his wife died in childbirth and the child did not survive. He was heart-broken but looked to our Saviour for comfort. Thereafter he devoted his life to the service of our Lord. He cared with great devotion for his parents, both of whom passed away a few years ago."

"Were there any strangers about in the last few weeks?"

Owain thought for a moment and then the unfortunate Claudius suddenly came to mind.

"The only stranger in these parts was a man from eastern Gaul called Claudius.

"One day on our way back from the port at Tregaran, we found him lying exhausted on the highway verge. He said he had come from his home village, when it was invaded by the warlike Alani and he and his companions were driven out. They were journeying towards Armorica, but he became separated from his group, after an attack by bandits. We took him home with us and fed him for a few days. He left early one morning, just leaving a short note thanking us. The note said that he had dreamt that his companions were near."

"It seems strange that he left in that way. What impression did you have of him?"

"He seemed to me like a soul in trouble, whom I needed to help. My steward and companion at the time, Ifor, was a little suspicious, not for any particular reason. Ifor, who has served as my steward since we moved here, is a bit of a sceptic at times."

"Was there anything unusual or noticeable about the behaviour of this Claudius?"

"Not really…except that he kept his bags very close to him and would not allow us to carry them for him, when we first found him. He explained they contained his father's few possessions which they had managed to take from their village. He felt that they were very precious to him. His father had died during the Alani raid."

"Did he ever have any disagreement with Emyr or was he hostile to the Church of our Lord?"

"I saw no sign of anything like that. I do not think he ever even met Emyr. We never talked about the Faith. He was with us for a very short time."

"The acorns found on the body might be a clue of some kind. Could they just have fallen from the trees or did someone, perhaps the killer, put them there for a reason?"

"I don't know about a reason but I am told they were in a neat pile. We don't think they just fell from the trees. According to the shepherds, they looked as if they had been carefully placed in a pile there near his heart."

"The only thought I have had is that acorns are said to be a symbol used by the Druids. As they were reported to be in a pile and not just scattered, it looks as if someone put them there as a sign of some sort."

"Do you think that this dreadful deed could possibly have been carried out by the Druids, as an attack on our religion?"

"I do not believe so and I sincerely hope not, as there have been friendly enough relations between our religions for many years in this region. The Druids and other pagans went undercover when all religions other than the true Faith were banned by the Emperor Theodosius in the last century. They kept themselves to themselves, but I am told that they celebrated the solstices and the spring festival in their traditional locations. This did not trouble our community and indeed we respected the Druids' knowledge of traditional medical remedies and of astrology. We still do.

"We have tried to convert them to our Faith, and some of them and their followers have indeed abandoned their paganism for the true religion. There are many converts in the vicinity of Condate, thanks mainly to the efforts of our most devout senior bishop.

"Soon we are to visit the very wise Abbot Clement at the abbey. He has a wide knowledge of all communities in the region, and would probably know of any animosity between the Druids or other pagans towards us. I will ask for his advice on such matters and about this foul murder."

"I think we will have to leave it there for the moment. But your help and that of the abbot will be greatly valued. In the meantime, we have advised our community to take care when travelling—not to travel alone and to avoid travel after dark. We do not normally carry weapons but for the time being some of us will do so. I and others have experience of warfare and the use of weapons, having had to defend ourselves from the various pagans when in Britannia. Most of us have swords and spears which we keep at home, in case of any trouble."

Chapter 5
Visit to the Abbey

Owain and Joseph then joined Gwen and the others for refreshment.

Gwen, still her ever amiable self, said in slightly agitated tones, "That took you a long time. These young men have good appetites and could easily have finished off all the food. But I kept some for you both, as well as some of our excellent cider."

There was a good spread on the table with fine crusty bread, fresh butter, some cheeses, cold ham and cold pork and relishes as well as beer and cider. There were also sweet pastries and cakes which Gwen had made with help from her capable daughter, Morwenna.

Owain explained that they had been discussing in some detail the terrible crime which had been committed.

"I wanted to acquaint the Presbyter with all the facts and circumstances, so far as we know them and to obtain his guidance as to how this foul murder might have come about. He has kindly confirmed that he will give his attention to it and discuss it with the venerable abbot. There must be information somewhere that would help solve this awful mystery."

The next day, Joseph and Luke departed on their journey, leaving Daniel and Matthew at Trepunek. They headed south to Ponterle to pay a visit to the abbey. Owain spent the rest of that day talking to Daniel, telling him in detail about the town, the area and some of the local personalities. Owain soon appreciated that Daniel was very different from Emyr, perhaps a little austere, but very learned and scholarly. He certainly knew his Bible very well. Owain concluded that Daniel would serve the local community with great devotion, and guide them like a good shepherd. He felt relieved to be reconnected with the Catholic Church.

This was also the time when Gwen had introduced Matthew to their children, including their daughter, Morwenna. She was just seventeen and stunningly beautiful, in the full bloom of youth. She was slim and elegant with gorgeous long dark hair tied back with a red ribbon, and stunningly beautiful dark eyes. The young horseman Matthew could not take his eyes off her. When he tried to speak, he was tongue-tied. All he could manage was, "Hello, I'm Matthew." But it was a start. Gwen saw that he was just a bit shy, but thought he was very nice-looking and most polite. She gave him an affectionate smile. Morwenna thought that Luke, whom she had seen a little earlier, was the more handsome of the two and also obviously very sensitive, but she also liked Matthew very much. She thought that Luke was the more smartly dressed with his fine dark red tunic and brown cloak.

When Joseph and Luke arrived at the abbey, they were met there by Clement, the abbot, and some of the brothers. They were given a very warm welcome; this may partly be due to the fact that the establishment was relatively new and less well known than other older monasteries. Visitors were rare and it was always very pleasing to the abbot to be asked to show visitors around, the more so when they included a potential new member.

They were given a tour around the monastery which lasted for almost two hours: its spacious dining hall, its kitchen, its workshops, its stables, its chapel and its grounds. It was what might be called a plain and simple place, with a peaceful and holy atmosphere. The visitors could not fail to be impressed. Joseph wondered how much it must all have cost, even if some of the work was carried out by the monks themselves. Joseph did not ask that question but Clement may have guessed what was in his thoughts, and so he expressed his gratitude for the generous funding which the foundation had received from several wealthy patrons and from the Bishop of Augustobona Tricassia[22].

Luke, from a farming background, was particularly interested in the vegetable garden and farm which were being set up. There was even a vineyard. The land had a slight slope towards the south and the grounds were in full sunlight most of the day. There was a pleasant stream nearby for irrigation, when needed, and there were two abundant springs for drinking water. Everything there was so neatly tended; the vines, their supports, the hedges and ditches, the orchards, the arable fields and the pastures. He noticed that many of the outbuildings were covered in honeysuckle, which added to their attraction and

---

[22] Troyes, France

prevented them from looking austere. Luke concluded that a very favoured site had been chosen for this holy project, and he was beginning to believe that it was surely a place where he was meant to spend his days serving the Lord.

Joseph had rather to spoil the tranquillity of the scene by telling Clement the tragic story of the death of Deacon Emyr. The abbot was moved to tears. He had not previously heard of this event and the news came as a shock to him. He had met Emyr on a number of occasions, both at the abbey and at Condate. He had great admiration for this very pious and devoted deacon. His grief at the news of his death and indeed his murder was hard for Clement to bear.

When he had composed himself, he focused on the pile of acorns.

"It is known that this is a Druidic symbol traditionally used in the west of Armorica. In the past there have been troubles with Druidic followers and other pagans. There has even been violence but nothing like the cold-blooded murder of an unarmed man, which you have described. Through our charitable work we are well respected by the small pagan communities which still exist. They know we come in peace and will help those in poverty or other difficulties. We aim to convert non-believers, but not to the extent of being domineering. If the seed falls on fertile ground, it will germinate and grow. Sometimes, it can land on thick thorns."

Joseph smiled knowingly, as a man with similar experience. He then added, with a sympathetic smile, "I have met thick thorns many times and stony ground. But that makes success the sweeter when we see souls converted."

Clement gave an equally knowing smile again. He added, "I will ask Brother James, who was born in this area and who knows many of the local people, to make some enquiries when he is on his rounds. Migrants have come to our region not just to escape the Saxons and other invaders in Britannia but also from eastern Gaul driven out by the Vandals, the Goths and other invaders.

"I am told by the Bishop of Autissiodorum that the Salian Franks are becoming ever more powerful in the east of Gaul. Attempts to convert their leaders to the faith have so far failed. All this awful conflict leads to migration. Amongst the migrants, there is, I am sorry to say, a small criminal element, which has sought opportunities in the turmoil and disruption caused by invaders for nefarious deeds, including theft, robbery, abduction and rape.

"It is just possible that such men may have been involved in the tragic event of which you have told us."

Joseph responded, "We do indeed live in troubled times, since the Romans lost control of the Empire. It is worrying to think of criminal gangs being abroad, especially if they have murderous inclinations."

The abbot and Joseph then had a slightly more relaxed conversation about the state of the world. They were both knowledgeable about political and secular matters as well as spiritual ones, and discussed how matters might end up.

Joseph began the conversation, "Yes, we live in troubles times. This really is the age of migration. I am an example of this myself, having migrated to Gaul with my parents when I was a lad. In the same way many people in Armorica came here from Britannia, and particularly from the south-west of that land."

The abbot pointed out, "There was always movement of people within the Roman Empire, as Roman citizenship had been bestowed upon most freemen. There were no borders within the Empire and there was scope for trade. But the migration in our age has been quite different, being in the nature of hostile invasions. As the Western Roman Empire became less well defended, invasions took place. As you will know, Joseph, the River Rhenus and the Danubius had been the boundaries of the Empire and in better times had been well defended."

Joseph nodded in agreement, having studied Roman history. He added, "The tribes from Germania crossed the Rhenus into Gaul at the beginning of this century and the Huns under Attila also invaded Gaul. This forced the Romans to take their legions from Britannia to try to defend Gaul and restore peace. But it led to invasions of Britannia by the Saxons and other infidels."

The abbot added, "The dreadful Huns from Asia had also driven the Goths from their homeland and they too arrived in the Roman Empire, and ended up driving the Vandals out of Hispania. The Vandals in turn migrated to North Africa. The most powerful migrants into Gaul seem to be the Salian Franks, who seem to have ambitions to conquer the whole of Gaul."

Joseph responded, "We are living in dangerous and unpredictable times, but the status of the Catholic Church is a cause of hope, not only our powerful message from the Gospels, but also in terms of administration, scholarship and learning."

"You are quite right about that and I hope and trust that our new abbey here can play its part in bringing peace and stability in Armorica and further afield."

"God willing, I firmly believe it will. But what has happened to Luke? When I last saw him, he was in the stables."

"He then went all over the farm and the garden full of enthusiasm, and I expect he is still there somewhere."

The abbot was correct and they then went over and joined Luke, who expressed his pleasure at seeing all the facilities of the abbey.

Chapter 6
Matthew and Luke

In the year 461, on an extensive farming estate near Condate, two young men were resting after a hard day's work in the fields. Their young faces looked weathered by the sun and wind, and their hair was dishevelled. As they relaxed at the farmhouse, they watched the sun setting over the beech woodlands to the west of the city. They loved the sunset for its own beauty but also it was a sign that supper was on its way. They also watched a gaggle of wild geese flying over the outer pasture lands, with their strident and insistent calls. They were also probably on their way home for supper on some distant lake.

Being young, having worked hard all day and being in the bracing fresh air, the young men were hungry and were picking up the enticing smells of freshly baked bread and of meat on the spit. Supper was still at little way off and they spent the time discussing a variety of subjects, such as last year's excellent harvest, the further reported migrations into Gaul by Germanic tribes, and their recent visit to Trepunek. As they turned to that subject, Matthew did not seem quite himself. Luke knew his cousin well enough to pick up that he had been a little moody at times in recent weeks. This was apparent to Luke now.

Tentatively, Luke looked at Matthew, trying to gauge his state of mind and asked: "Is everything okay, Matt? At times, you look a little lost in your thoughts. Are you worried, like me, whether our families' lands might be taken by Goths or Franks or others, or is it something else?"

Matthew did not respond for a moment, but was deep in thought.

Luke looked kindly at his dear cousin and said, "If it helps, do tell me what's troubling you. But if this is not quite the right time, not to worry."

"I've been thinking over your wish to enter monastic life, and doing so over and over again; I was wondering whether I should not want to do the same. But recently I have been thinking about girls too much. I have been having thoughts which have made me feel sort of ashamed. It all started at Trepunek, when we met Owain's daughter, Morwenna. I have met pretty girls before, but no one quite like her. She is so beautiful and charming."

Matthew struggled to find the words to express his feelings and then continued.

"I have found girls attractive before, but this is different. I can't get her out of my mind. I thought of writing to her, as Owain had said that all his children can read and write. But I don't know what she thinks of me. I don't want to make a fool of myself. I really want to go back there and see her, but I don't know whether that will ever be possible. In the meantime, I just do not know what to do. I have never felt like this before, but I am glad I have told you about it. We have always been best friend and it's good if we can talk about things."

Luke listened sympathetically, but was worried, not only about Matthew's very normal feelings but also about his own. Whilst in the very short period of time he had seen her, although he had found Morwenna nice-looking and charming, he felt no sexual attraction to her at all. Whilst Matthew might be guilty at the very worst of youthful lecherous thoughts, he knew that his own feelings were much worse, finding boys and men sexually attractive. This had happened to him ever since early puberty, and he was shocked by and ashamed of these feelings. He was only too aware that such desires were contrary to the teachings of the Bible, especially if they were to lead to any action driven on by such sinful urges.

He thought carefully about what to say in reply. This was not yet the time to admit his own feelings, but he wanted to help his cousin. He spoke to Matthew in a rather formal and almost priest-like way, but with affection at the same time, "I do not think it is a sin to find girls attractive. Men and women fall in love with each other all the time and a happy marriage can follow. We know that St Paul approves of Christian marriage. My advice to you is that when you next attend confession is to tell the priest how you feel and how you want to do the righteous thing. He will have heard similar confessions many times before and I am sure he will be able to help you. You never know: you might get to meet Morwenna again and she might also like you. You are a very eligible bloke from a good family. Don't give up hope."

"Thank you for that, Luke. Confession is obviously something I should have considered but it had not crossed my mind. I will, however, tell of my feelings, if I can get up the courage, at my next confession. I won't give up hope about her but I am afraid it is just hope."

Matthew felt better firstly at having got things off his chest and at thinking about confession.

The conversation, however, made Luke feel quite disconcerted, when he thought of his deep-seated homosexual inclinations. *Should I tell of these at confession or would I feel too ashamed? Could the confessor give me any sort of comfort or advice? Could I ever bring myself to tell Matt and my parents?*

He was in a dilemma of the sort which may have faced many young men in the early Christian era. In classical times homosexuality was regarded as normal. Even Julius Caesar 'swung both ways', or so they say. In Plato's Symposium, which deals with love in all its forms, sexual love between males is highly regarded. Luke, one might say, was born five hundred years too late.

He was a conscientious young man and was deep in thought, *Was my wish to go into a monastery motivated not just by a wish to serve the Lord but also to be in male company, where I might be tempted into carnal sin?* Luke did not show it, but he was in turmoil. His feelings and his beliefs were diametrically opposed and he knew it only too well. He did not feel able to talk to anyone about it.

Supper was ready and the two young men joined their families for the excellent meal of roast pork with a spicy apple relish home-made in line with an old Roman recipe. They were both troubled in their different ways about their feelings: all part of the difficult business of growing up. After their serious discussion, Matthew's mood and appetite was rather better than that of his cousin. The next day they both worked hard on the farm. Such activity and the healthy fatigue which it brought on helped them both to feel less stressed, at least for a time. But strong feelings and desires cannot be completely repressed for long.

Chapter 7
Owain Goes to Market

It was springtime at Trepunek in the year 461, and its tranquil life and activities went on as usual. Daniel officiated much as his predecessor had done at the Eucharist. His sermons were more scholarly than those of Emyr, but the general message was much the same; about charity in thought and deed and caring for others.

Seasonal work went on at the farms, including Owain's. Men went hunting and fishing, full of hope and enthusiasm. Women and girls spent time weaving, spinning and sewing. Millers ground corn to make bread flour. Some boys studied Latin and other subjects at the abbey. Sometimes the local militia met on the common land to train and hone their skills on horseback and with weapons. There were several well-organised militias in Armorica, which were all linked together and coordinated by the ruling families of the area. It was said that all these families were related to the first Celtic ruler of Armorica, a noble warrior called Conan Meriadoc. The militiamen hoped that they would not need to fight in wars, but the rulers and military leaders knew that the situation in much of Gaul was unstable, now that the Pax Romana, which had provided security for all, was at an end. There was also the threat from highwaymen, pirates and common criminals, not to mention the Visigoths and the Salian Franks.

Owain's boys attended the Abbey at Ponterle each term for instruction in theology, Latin and rhetoric. They also helped in the gardens there, improving their horticultural skills. Kitto was the better of the two at academic studies, but Tomos had a natural aptitude in horticulture. He was keen to learn from the knowledgeable monks all about this.

The monthly market took place in Trepunek, with produce of all kinds offered for sale, including clothing and footwear, and sometimes swords and weapons of war or for hunting. Often musicians and singers performed for the entertainment of the public at these lively events. People attended from farms and homes from miles around.

One day, having returned from the market, Owain was in particularly good spirits. His produce had sold well and he had also purchased a stout pair of boots for himself and some fine jewellery for Gwen.

When he arrived home, Gwen greeted him with obvious enthusiasm, "You'll never guess what. A sealed package has just been brought here from the port. The messenger said that it was sent from Cornubia. It might be a reply from Teged. Here it is."

She handed it to him as if it was the most precious thing in the world.

Owain shared her hopes that it was from his dear brother. He unpacked and opened it with the utmost care. It was indeed from his brother, Teged, who was now in Cornubia with his family and household. Owain was shaking slightly as he read the letter. It stated that Teged and his family would be crossing to Armorica the very next week. This was incredibly exciting news. He had received no prior warning that Teged had decided to migrate. It all came as a delightful surprise. Owain and Gwen were both filled with joy, and could hardly contain themselves whilst waiting for the next week. They each celebrated with a goblet of their very best wine from southern Gaul.

Throughout history, migration has taken place. Migrants have come in all shapes and sizes, and with a wide range of wealth from utter poverty to riches. The Hebrews migrated to Egypt and the holy family did the same as refugees from King Herod. Some migrants have travelled in large groups, even in tribes. Others go alone or perhaps a group of a few desperate folk. Some are people fleeing wars or famine, and travel only with the clothes they stand in. Some come as invaders armed to the teeth, intending to pillage and abduct humans, or to take over land and then settle.

Many of the Britons migrating to Armorica were poor, whether by birth or as a result of having to flee for their lives when attacked by Saxon raiders. Such people managed to cross the sea to their new home, with help from others including ships' captains. There were communities of poor residents having to restart their lives from scratch, with help from others already there or from the institutions of the Christian Church. In time, some of them would manage to build new lives and prosper. In turn, they might help other new immigrants.

Teged and his family were in the rarer category of the wealthy Romano-Britons, able to migrate at their own time of choosing, and to travel to a place where they would expect a warm welcome. Apart from his inherited wealth, Teged was a very skilled and successful horse-breeder and horse-trader. These lucrative activities he would be leaving behind, but he hoped to start up again in Armorica, where he thought that there would surely be a market for horses of various kinds and for diverse uses, and perhaps with better opportunities to carry on horse-trading with other peoples.

Teged had chartered a sizeable galleon to convey the family, their servants, their slaves, their horses and other animals to their new home. Owain and Teged were from a noble family which was part of the powerful British Cornovii tribe[23]. Some parts of this tribe had in the past migrated to south-west Britain to help drive out Hibernian settlers from the coastal areas. Some say that the Romans named Cornubia after this tribe. Teged brought with him many gold and silver coins and a large collection of weapons. He also had a collection of musical instruments. Amongst the animals on the ship were Teged's two well-trained sheepdogs.

One of his company of migrants was a mature uncle, called Maldwyn, who was very knowledgeable about the history of Britannia, and could always entertain any company with his stories. He had been unusually quiet on the voyage. Some would say that was a bonus. There was no more than a moderate swell on the open sea, but it was too much for Maldwyn, who discovered that he was not a good sailor. He was very relieved to set foot on dry land in Armorica. Very soon his full vocal prowess would return in all its glory, and the great storyteller would continue to inform and amuse. It was a big wrench for Maldwyn to leave his homeland at his age, but he was very close to Teged and Sioned and would have felt lost without them.

Teged had very different looks from those of his brother. He was taller and slim with dark hair and brown eyes. He did smile at times but usually had a serious look on his face. He had fought with distinction in a militia in Britannia but he was mainly a farmer and horse-breeder. He had the look of a business man: someone who was always on the ball, and looking for opportunities. Owain on the other hand looked as if everything in the world was rosy. In those days that certainly was not the case in much of the world.

Teged's wife, Sioned, was a quiet person and some might say introverted, but that would be doing her an injustice. She was, in fact, a devout Christian and

---

[23] The Cornovii were a British tribe based in what is now the Powys and Shropshire region

a spiritual person in the broadest sense. At times, when asked, she would sit with a sick person, who would feel comforted by her presence. She was also someone often called upon to sit with a dying person to be with them when they passed away. That was a special quality valued in Celtic societies. Sioned was not beautiful in the way of her sister-in-law, Gwen, who was a brunette with sparkling brown eyes. Sioned had a pleasant and appealing face and manner, and was well liked. She was a loyal and faithful wife and a caring mother.

Chapter 8
The Arrival

As one might expect, there was a grand and joyous celebration for Teged and his family following their arrival at Trepunek. As well as his loving wife, Sioned, there were his two sons, Geraint and Cadwur, and his daughter, Nessa. They had produced other offspring who had sadly died in infancy, as often happened in those days. Geraint was cut out to be a farmer. He resembled his uncle Owain in looks, without having the regular smile on his round face. Cadwur looked like his dad, Teged, and was a chip off the old block. He was strong and athletic and had a liking for any weapon of war. Nessa loved horses and was always delighted to observe the birth of a foal and watch it taking its first faltering steps. She also enjoyed fighting with her brothers, in a robust but playful way. She could give a good account of herself.

Of all the family and household, Cadwur was the most sorry to leave his home country, mainly because, although still young, he hated the idea of the Saxons taking more land and felt a strong urge to stay and fight them. Teged sympathised with this view, but was persuaded by Owain's letter and by his own analysis of the situation that it was his duty to his family to take them to Armorica, where their chances of a safe and prosperous future were greater. Young Nessa looked forward to the adventure, so long as there would be horses in the new country. The eldest son, Geraint, was a peace-loving lad, more interested in farming than battles. He was content enough to move to Armorica.

The Presbyter Joseph, and the cousins Luke and Matthew, all from Condate, attended the celebration, along with many folk from Trepunek.

The culmination of festivities was a carousal, banquet and dance in a large barn, which had been cleared for the occasion, and then suitably decked out. After a sumptuous meal of seabass, lobster, salmon, venison, and pheasant followed by all kinds of delicacies, and washed down with fine wine, the dancing commenced.

There was a local band of musicians—playing flutes, lyres, lutes, drums and cymbals, and performing well-known Celtic melodies and dance music. There were also performances by various singers, including Owain's daughter, Morwenna. She was familiar with many of the traditional songs, and was blessed with a most beautiful voice. She impressed and delighted the audience, especially the young Matthew, who was now totally star-struck by her. A combination of beauty and grace, plus musical talent, was too much of this young farmer to cope with. Things got even more exciting when, in a traditional dance, Morwenna gave him an affectionate smile. Then during a dance movement they were able to hold hands for a moment, until it was time for them to separate and move on to other partners. Luke also participated as he loved music and dancing, but not for him, sadly, as an exciting pathway to the opposite sex.

As time progressed and the wheat, oats and barley grew, Matthew and Morwenna spent time together and became engaged, with permission from parents on both sides. In due course they were married, and Morwenna left Trepunek to live with her husband on his family's estate near Condate. She had all the skills necessary for a farmer's wife, everything from weaving, sewing and housework to tending to animals and weeding vegetable gardens. She also loved horses and was a fine rider. She played the lyre with great skill and knew many songs which she loved to sing. Although she missed her family, she was very happy with Matthew and really liked the city of Condate. Owain had provided a generous dowry of sheep and cattle.

On the first morning when Teged awoke in Armorica, he had seen a magnificent sunrise from the direction of Condate, with pinks and reds in the pale sky just above the horizon, more beautiful than the finest art work he had ever seen. It was like the rosy-fingered dawn as described in Homer's Odyssey in the Latin translation which he had been required to study at Deva. He had to confess that this sunrise was more beautiful than those he had experienced in Powys, where the hills were higher so that it was not normally possible to see the rising sun so low in the sky. He was sure that good times were ahead for him and his family.

Within a few days and with a strong feeling of optimism for his new land of Armorica, Teged purchased for a modest price a large semi-abandoned Roman villa in the countryside near Trepunek together with its grounds extending to well over a hundred and fifty acres. The Gallo-Roman family who owned it were all elderly and were pleased to sell it for a fair price, which enabled them to move to Condate to a much smaller home. Their sons and other relatives had moved to eastern Gaul to join or support a Roman garrison there.

The restoration of the villa and the ground was a major task, which kept Teged, his household and some hired workers many months to complete. Teged even had some new mosaics installed by some migrant workers from Britannia, who had learnt this skill from Roman artists. Even the elderly Uncle Maldwyn helped as much as he could, although he could be a mixed blessing, as he kept talking and telling stories to those working around him.

Teged had to complain:-

"Dear Uncle Maldwyn, as much as we love you and enjoy your stories, we need to make progress. There is just too much laughing and too little work."

Maldwyn was contrite and promised to mend his ways, but later on it all started up again. By then things had moved on with the building work, and Teged wisely decided to let matters take their course. Perhaps his uncle was keeping the workers amused, cheerful and motivated, and in his own way was moving matters along.

Within about a year, Teged had established a fine home for his family and household and a sizeable working farm. His brother's description in his letter of life in Armorica was proving to be accurate. The region was peaceful, the land was fertile and there were plenty of good places for hunting and fishing. Teged also made a start on the business of breeding horses. His daughter Nessa was always very keen to help with that activity, or anything to do with horses.

He had been told of the awful murder of Deacon Emyr, but, like others, concluded that this was an unexplained and isolated incident.

Teged was well aware that there were Celtic rulers of the regions of Armorica and there was a High King, as was the case in Britannia, but it seemed that, in Armorica, these rulers worked together in view of the threat from the last remnants of the Roman forces, the Goths, the Franks, the Vandals and other Germanic tribes. With a large coastline, there was also always the risk of pirates landing and making damaging raids. The people of Armorica knew they had to defend themselves against all hostile forces and were prepared and organised to do so.

Chapter 9
Luke Goes to the Abbey

In the year 461, after much heart searching and studying of religious texts, Luke made the firm decision to become a monk at Ponterle. He felt that the religious life, along with the academic studies which went with it, would provide all he needed for a fulfilled life. In addition there was the bonus of the gardens and farm, where he could perform a useful role in the corporate life of the abbey. There was something about the abbey and its grounds which appealed to Luke at a very deep spiritual level. To him it was almost like the Garden of Eden, a world of simplicity and innocence, a place on Earth close to Heaven.

His mother and father had mixed feelings about his decision. They were both devout people and realised how committed their son was to doing God's work. At the same time, they would sorely miss him and he would be a loss to their farm, as they had only one other son, who was several years younger than Luke and who had never enjoyed good health. Matthew was, of course, still available to share the work, and they had an ample number of servants and slaves.

Luke never dared to mention his sexuality to his parents nor to confess it to the confessor. He convinced himself that with God's help he would be pure in thought and deed and would never give in to temptation.

His first year as a novice went exceptionally well. He was an exemplary pupil, diligent in prayer, in studying Latin and in working as a scribe under close and scholarly supervision. In outdoor work, he was both skilled and conscientious, and needed little guidance. He was also physically fit and strong for his age. He much enjoyed fresh air and physical activity. He loved the abbey and, although he missed his parents and Matthew, he felt it was his home.

Abbot Clement was delighted with his attitude and progress. Luke had, for example, made a very accurate copy of part of 'the City of God', a momentous work in Latin by the great Bishop Augustine of Hippo. In theology, Luke became an expert in the Arian controversy, and in the arguments against Gnosticism and Pelagianism, the latter a heresy which had been rife in Britannia.

It was an easy decision to promote him to the rank of a monk. His parents and also Matthew, his cousin, were told of his success and were delighted for him.

As a monk, his progress continued and he became a much valued member of the community. But, although outwardly everything seemed good and normal, internally at times he was in turmoil, particularly at night when he lay on his bunk. He could not help thinking about boys and young men, who were so near to him and yet so far away. He wondered what it would be like to hold a young man in his arms and embrace him. He felt thoroughly ashamed at such thoughts and asked for God's forgiveness. At confession, he never dared to mention these feelings and hoped they would simply go away.

There was one week when his task was to make a copy of the Book of Leviticus from one of the abbey's illustrated copies of the Latin Vulgate Bible. This included verses from Chapters 18 and 20.

"You shall not lie with a male as with a woman; it is an abomination."
"If a man lies with a male as with a woman, both have committed an abomination; they should surely be put to death; their blood is upon them."

These verses were not new to Luke, but the act of writing them out in the course of his duties as a monk brought home to him the enormity of his dilemma. He was well aware too of the passages in the New Testament Letter of St Paul to the Romans about homosexuality. He was in a battle which he had to win. His emotions were almost too much to bear and he turned to prayer for comfort.

He tried harder than ever to be pure in thought and deed. His desire to remain pure and resist temptation was a regular part of his prayers. Nothing in the way he looked or behaved gave any indication of his feelings and no one could possibly have imagined how he felt. For much of the time, he was busy with study or works of various kinds and his sexual feelings were pushed to the very back of his mind.

Chapter 10
To the Woods

Time had moved on for Luke and it was now autumn in the Year of our Lord 464. One of the important jobs at the abbey at this time of year was to collect firewood for the winter from nearby woods and forests. The brother in charge of this task was Amos, who was in his tenth year of monastic service. He was chosen for this duty as he was tall and strong with a fine physique, and very experienced as a forester. There was no one better in the use of axes and saws. He needed an assistant to help in sawing and chopping wood, and to help with the large and cumbersome horse-drawn cart, which he used in this type of work. Amos was a gentle giant: tall and muscular but with an amiable face and clear blue eyes.

At the time of his first outing in the year in question, his usual assistant was unwell and Luke was given the task of helping Amos. Luke too was physically strong, having carried out farm work from an early age and now having matured into an adult. He knew how to take charge of a horse-drawn cart whether the route was on a good road or over rough tracks.

And so one fine morning the two brothers left together on the cart containing their specially prepared and sharpened tools and equipment. They also took drinking water and a packed lunch for themselves, as the job would last all day. As they were departing, a young monk with whom Luke was on friendly terms whispered to him, "Good luck, Brother Luke. Take care and mind your back."

Luke was a bit puzzled by these remarks but assumed that they were a reflection of the fact that the work was potentially hazardous. He replied, "Thank you, Zeb. I will be very careful."

When they reached the chosen part of the wood, Amos stripped down for work, removing his habit and wearing just his undergarments. His powerful arms and strong chest muscles were apparent. Luke followed suit, as he too was expecting to carry out hard physical work.

The smaller trees could not resist the mighty blows from Amos' large axe. For larger trees they worked together with a two-man saw. This was an exhausting activity and regular breaks were needed. They felled several poplars, which must each have been eighty feet tall. Luke was anxious when they started work on the first poplar, as he feared it might fall on them. Amos, seeing the look on his colleague's face, assured him that all would be well, as he would cut at the correct angle to ensure that the trees would fall away from them. He also said, "Poplars are soft wood and much easier to fell than oaks." The poplars were felled successfully and the couple left them on the ground to be cut up later on.

It was now midday and the pair rested, after a hard morning's work, and took lunch in a grassy glade in dappled shade, hidden away in a remote part of the wood. Luke thought it was a wonderful spot, with the surrounding deciduous trees in their late autumn colours and with fallen leaves all around. There were also the smells of autumn with damp leaves, grasses and earth. There were snaking tree roots to be seen and unearthly looking fungi all around.

Amos said Grace, and Luke joined in with an Amen. When they had eaten and enjoyed the simple fare and quenched their thirst with water, they lay down and appreciated the warmth and mellow light of the gentle autumn sunshine finding its way through the leafy cover. All they could hear in this idyllic spot was birdsong, including that of the nightingale, some nearby and some distant, together with the faint gurgling of the River Evorn[24] at the far side of the wood down in a shallow gorge.

Luke could not take his eyes off his colleague, with admiration for his physique and strength. Amos had seen that look from young men many times before and sensed what Luke was feeling. The two looked at each other in a way which showed affection and desire.

Amos spoke tenderly to his young and handsome colleague, "You are a strong and good-looking lad, Luke. There is a look of desire in your eyes, which you can't disguise. Your eyes are showing me what you want, what you yearn for. I can show you how good love-making can be, if you come into my arms and let me hold you tenderly. I guess it would be your first time to feel a man inside you. I will be gentle and show you the way."

---

[24] A fictional river

With that he lent over Luke and caressed his face, all the time making eye contact. Luke felt powerless and totally under Amos' control, but also with excitement and expectation which overwhelmed him. Luke was physically strong enough to resist if he wanted to, but he just wanted to surrender and let matters take their course, with Amos doing what he wanted to do. His long resistance to his sexual feelings broke, just like a dam. He could no longer fight against his deepest desires. The two men kissed tenderly and Amos whispered, "Sweet boy. It's wonderful to kiss your lovely lips. Shall we go on all the way?" The two men continued kissing tenderly and then the love-making progressed. Luke was experiencing a taste of ecstasy.

Luke found Amos very handsome with such a fine and powerful physique but at the same time with the most beautiful blue eyes, and also so loving and tender. Their love-making was passionate and performed in a way strictly prohibited in the scriptures, which they both knew well. When they had both reached a climax, they laid in each-others' arms until the physical pleasure of their union slowly abated.

Then Luke's heart was filled with terrible shame, as if he had been stabbed in the heart or he had been burnt with hot metal. With tears in his eyes and full of shame and remorse, he forced himself to speak, "What we have done, dear Brother Amos, is a terrible, terrible sin."

Tears continued to fill his eyes but he could say no more. He then recalled the advice from a fellow monk that morning to take care and mind his back. Perhaps that young monk was speaking from similar experience.

Amos' only response was a warm smile and shrug of his broad shoulders. They then put on and adjusted their clothing and went back to work, almost as if nothing had happened. To Amos, what had happened was a wonderful and delightful experience, but for Luke he was shaken to his very essence. The heavy work, however, just went on.

They spent some hours chopping up the fallen trees and branches, and then loaded up the cart. The job of managing the bulky and fully laden cart on its journey back to the abbey was tiring, especially for Luke after a hard day's physical work plus the traumatic episode at lunchtime.

They unloaded the wood into the large covered store at the abbey and received deserved thanks from the abbot for their hard work. Amos led the horse back to the stables. The abbot would have been utterly shocked if he knew everything that had happened on that autumn day.

The weather stayed fine and warm for the time of year and Amos and Luke went back to the wood on each of the next few days. Luke tried hard to repress his feelings for Amos, but on the fifth day he gave in and they made love again in the same remote glade.

Luke felt overwhelmed and desperate. Again he felt ecstatic from the physical union but at the same time totally ashamed of his sinful conduct. He just said, "This is a terrible sin. I feel so guilty. I have turned my back on God."

This time Amos felt the need to respond, "Dear Luke, you might like to know that I have had these feelings all my life. When I was just sixteen, I was in an arranged marriage with a young girl of about my age. We had sex a few times but it was no good at all for me. It almost seemed like an unnatural thing for me. We just did not get on at all in any way and she got to dislike me intensely. I was young and irresponsible and could not handle it. I just abandoned her, left home and went travelling. I was in a militia for a while and fought in a few skirmishes against isolated groups of Goths and others. I also did some forestry work, which is where I learnt my skills in what we have been doing today.

"I have always been a Christian. My family taught me to read Latin and I studied the Bible with guidance from a deacon of the church. Later I went to the monastery founded by Abbot Martin at Caesarodonum[25] and asked if I could do paid work as a forester. Eventually I was admitted as a novice and remained there until our abbey was founded by Clement. I transferred here as they needed a forester and I have been here since then. I know full well that homosexual acts and indeed fornication with women are sins. Bishop Augustine tells us that man is born with original sin, and only through the Grace of God can we achieve redemption. He says that we must show love to sinners, who we all are.

"God made me with these feelings for other men. I hope he will forgive me for my sins. He could, if he had so chosen, have made me heterosexual."

Luke thought hard before replying. He realised that Amos had been very frank with him and was in his own rugged way a thoughtful and sincere person. He composed himself, having taken in what Amos had said. He then responded with candour, "To receive forgiveness one must confess one's sins and do penance, although I do not think I am courageous enough to tell my confessor the terrible sins I have committed. I am just left with an awful and overwhelming feeling of shame and guilt."

---

[25] Tours. Abbot Martin was canonised as St Martin of Tours

"Confess your sins silently to God. He is almighty and merciful. Like me you were born with these feelings and God will understand. Do not feel guilty for one moment because you really are not."

Luke, who was not at all convinced, and looking forlorn replied, "I hope God will forgive me. I don't think I can forgive myself."

Luke knew that he could not talk of these things at confession; apart from anything else it might get Amos as well as himself into trouble.

The next day, the weather broke and there was a severe storm, blown in from the western ocean. The winds were terrifyingly strong and there was constant heavy rain. These conditions lasted for three whole days. Roads, tracks, fields and some buildings were flooded. The collection of wood was postponed and most monks were given duties indoors. At the abbey, there was a roof leak which Luke and others had to repair. Amos was glad of the break from forestry, and also knew from experience that storm-force winds like those battering the area would do some of his work for him. There were bound to be fallen trees and branches in woods, forests and elsewhere. This proved to be correct.

Chapter 11
Where Had Brother Luke Gone?

On the fourth day, the weather cleared up and Amos and Luke were due to go out to the wood early that morning. But Luke could not be found. He had not been to early morning prayers or to breakfast. His colleagues checked that he was not still on his bunk, perhaps suffering from an ailment. He was not to be found there or anywhere. A whole day went by with people asking questions and looking everywhere, but he did not reappear. The abbot was gradually getting more worried, as Luke was known to be very conscientious and reliable. It was not like him just to disappear without saying a word to anyone. The abbot charged four monks with the task of going out to the surrounding area to see what information they might find. They came back empty handed and disconsolate, and so the mystery of the missing monk continued. Meanwhile Amos was sent off with another monk to carry on with the collection of much-needed wood.

A messenger was sent all the way to Condate to visit the bishops there and to ascertain whether Luke might have gone back home or left some sort of message with his family. Again nothing came to light. His parents and his cousin Matthew were desperately worried as to what might have happened to him. They felt that monasticism was his true vocation and that for him the abbey was a peaceful and fulfilling place. They could not begin to understand his unexplained absence. They had no idea of his homosexual inclinations, which he had always kept strictly to himself.

Just over a week from his disappearance, the mystery was solved in a very distressing way. Some fishermen, who were preparing to net eels on the River Evorn several miles from Ponterle, found a body, in the garb of a monk, in the reed bed beside the river. After all the recent heavy rain, the river level had been high and the body could have been washed there from a long way off. They were duly shocked at their discovery and passed on this sad information to the abbey. The body was identified as that of Brother Luke.

There was no evidence as to where or how he got into the river. The nearest part of the river to the abbey was close to the wood, where he and Amos had collected firewood for their community. Amos, who knew all about Luke's dilemma, was utterly distraught and suspected suicide. As the brother who had been with Luke for the most time over recent days, Amos was questioned about Luke's state of mind. He answered all the questions put to him without referring to the activities which had taken place between them, and without in any way suggesting that Luke was depressed or emotionally disturbed. Amos did not want to say anything which might deny Luke a proper burial. Other monks said that Luke had been behaving normally. It seemed that he was the last person to be thought of as potentially suicidal. It is a sad fact, however, that suicide is sometimes totally unexpected by those close to the deceased.

There were no signs on the body to suggest that he had been attacked. The cause of his death was clearly drowning but there was no evidence of foul play or of suicide. As no one could say that he had committed suicide, he was therefore entitled to a normal Christian burial, which took place in due course at the abbey. It was a most sombre occasion for the monks and for those of his family who attended. It was even more distressing in that his death was a mystery. Some suspected suicide but, apart from Brother Amos, no one would know of any possible reason for the sad and premature death of this young, talented and devout monk. This was a truly tragic loss to the abbey and to his family.

The devout Luke had left the abbey in the middle of that fateful night and made his way to the river, his heart filled with overwhelming shame. He could not come to terms with what he had done and what he might be tempted to do again. As he plunged into the cold waters fully clothed, he imagined that it was the River Jordan and that its waters were washing away his sins and preparing him for entry into the Kingdom of Heaven. His mouth and chest filled with the cloudy waters of the Evorn and he gave up the ghost.

Chapter 12
The Militia

At about the time of Luke's tragic demise, there were fears in Armorica of hostile incursions particularly by Goths or Franks into this region. There was warfare of various degrees of intensity over much of Gaul at this time and the rulers of Armorica feared that fighting might spill over into their lands. The powerful Visigoths were threatening the southern borders of Armorica and the warlike Franks who held the land to the east of Armorica were ever seeking to expand their territory. The leaders of the militias in Armorica were charged with finding recruits to train and in time to engage in active service, if that should be needed. Many volunteers came forward.

In Trepunek, the volunteers included Owain's eldest son, Kitto, who was now eighteen and was keen to join a militia, as was his cousin, Cadwur, (the son of Teged) who was of the same age. Owain and Teged respected their boys' sense of duty but had misgivings, as they themselves had been involved in bloody military action in the past. They knew that warfare in whatever form it took was not always a glorious and romantic adventure, but could involve injury, death and grief.

The athletic Cadwur was particularly keen to join a militia, as he was a fine horseman and hunter and was skilled with a spear and in archery. He was a born warrior and could not wait for the chance to join a militia. Kitto was influenced by his cousin's enthusiasm but at heart was more of a farmer than a hunter or warrior. He liked seeing crops growing and maturing and also tending to animals. Nevertheless, if there were a crisis from invasions, he wanted to play his part and to be well prepared and trained for that. He felt strongly patriotic towards Armorica, a land where he and his family had found refuge and a warm welcome, after their days in Britannia confronted by hostile forces. Tomos, the younger son of Owain, and Geraint, the elder son of Teged, decided not to join the militia, as their interest was solely in farming in all its aspects. Cadwur humorously reflected, "If we are ever invaded, those two farmers would be fearsome with their pitchforks, if anyone ever tried to damage their crops or animals."

Cadwur and Kitto were readily accepted as recruits and their training started in September after the time of harvest. Full of enthusiasm they went away to a training camp near Condate. It was situated in woodland with flat meadows nearby. The broad wood trees were just beginning to change to their autumn colours and some were shedding leaves. The officer in charge of the training and induction was called Flavius, a seasoned soldier of Gallo-Roman descent appointed by the ruler of the region. Matthew, the cousin of Luke, and son-in-law of Owain, also joined this training camp. His young and beautiful wife, Morwenna, was not altogether happy as she was now expecting their second child.

The training was hard and rigorous, in line with Flavius' background as a federate of the Roman army. There was training with all kinds of weapons, as well as field-craft, and fitness training. Recruits also had to learn all the military commands whether given verbally or by signals. For those with horses, there was also intensive cavalry training. Cadwur excelled at this, with the skills of a rider far more experienced than normal young men of his age. He even received praise from Flavius, which was very unusual from this seasoned warrior. Whilst he was never unfair in his remarks to recruits, he liked to avoid young soldiers getting above themselves. He could not help admiring Cadwur. This was a warrior in the making, the best he had ever seen.

At the end of three months at the camp, Kitto, Cadwur and Matthew had passed all the tests and challenges, and were enrolled as junior members of the militia. They returned to their homes but could be summoned for further exercises or for active service when required. Cadwur, as he worked at home and on the farm, could not wait to be called upon for military service, as he yearned to put his training into practice and show off his outstanding skills as a member of the cavalry.

Over the next few years, there were indeed some occasions when the militiamen were called up for action: usually when there were large groups of ruthless bandits causing trouble for farmers near Condate. These criminals were no match for a well-organised and heavily armed militia. The cavalry in particular put the fear of God into them and those that were not slain wasted no time in running back eastward from whence they had come. On the first such mission, Cadwur proved to be the fearsome cavalier predicted by Flavius. It was Cadwur who killed the leader of the bandit group.

Afterwards, as the militia were discussing with Flavius how the day had gone and where there might be scope for improvement, Cadwur had some feelings of regret at having killed another human being. He was fully aware that this was the task of a soldier, but even so he felt uneasy. Perhaps it came from his Christian upbringing, with emphasis on loving your enemies. He knew that he had not acted wrongly, as he was defending local law-abiding citizens from theft or injury or worse, at the hands of these outlaws. He came to the conclusion that he was doing a necessary job, but at the same time he did not take pride or delight in the act of killing another human. It was an issue which many soldiers have faced throughout history, especially since the early days of Christendom and the teachings of the New Testament. *When war comes*, Cadwur thought, *there is often no choice. It's either him or me.*

A far more serious event led to a call up of the militia in 467, when there was an incursion by a small army of Franks near the borders of Armorica. They had arrived as a reconnaissance mission (on their own initiative and not as part of any plan by the rulers of the Franks to test out the defences of the region). But if they saw an opportunity, they would try to take territory. They were well trained and carried excellent weapons, but were mainly infantry, with some charioteers.

There followed a pitched battle in which they were confronted by the militia led by Flavius, with cavalry and a large infantry section. Both sides fought hard but the Franks were no match for the Armorican cavalry, who swung the conflict in favour of the Armoricans. Cadwur was again fearsome in battle and killed several opposition fighters, wounding and severing limbs with his mighty sword. Those of the Franks who survived escaped to eastern Gaul as quickly as they could. They took back the message that the east of Armorica was well defended and was not a pushover for invaders.

Both sides took losses, far less so on the Armorican side. Matthew and Cadwur came away unscathed but Kitto was not so fortunate. He sustained a serious leg injury from an enemy spear and lost a lot of blood. Although he survived the battle, it was deemed necessary for his leg to be amputated above the knee. This excruciatingly painful operation was carried out at Condate by a skilled surgeon, and was as successful as it could be. Kitto's life could was never be the same again. He could just about walk on crutches, but could do little on the family farm and certainly could never be part of the militia again. His family gave him all the sympathy and support they could but his father, Owain, knew that all soldiers face these risks to defend their territory. Sadly a year later Kitto's leg became badly infected and gangrene set in. He died shortly afterwards.

The grief which Owain and Gwen felt at this loss was unbearable. Tomos too was distraught, but was not one to show is feelings in an obvious way. He coped by applying himself to work on the farm with renewed vigour. He had always loved and respected his older brother, whom he thought to be far more intelligent than he and who had always supported him in all he did. Cadwur, Morwenna and Matthew also grieved deeply for Kitto. Gwen never got over the death of her son: Owain felt the irony of migrating to a safer land only to lose his first-born son to a battle wound.

Cadwur and Matthew, despite their heart-felt grief for Kitto, carried on in the militia and took part in many more skirmishes or battles; and both excelled and were promoted within the militia. When not fighting or training, they were available for farm work, and also much enjoyed a day of hunting, especially for wild boar, a formidable foe for hunters. Even the bold Cadwur took care when chasing one of these beasts. There was great delight when these hunters came back to their homes with a wild boar or a stag. The animal would be skilfully butchered and would provide rich suppers for whole families and their servants for some days. There were many traditional Celtic songs about hunting, which were often sung as these suppers were enjoyed. As well as hunting, there were those men and lads who specialised in trapping birds, both large and small, which made a welcome addition to the diet of the local people. This practice did not however have the excitement and panache of the hunt. There were no songs at those times about trapping birds.

Chapter 13
When Cadwur Met Rhian

In the Year of our Lord 467, there was another significant event in the town: a new family had arrived in Trepunek from Britannia. They were part of a mass migration to all parts of Gaul from their homeland in that decade, following the migration of more and more Saxons into Britannia. The family had made the perilous journey from Luguvalium,[26] a former Roman stronghold in the north of the country at the western end of Hadrian's Wall. They had come by sea from there to Trevena[27] on the north coast of Cornubia, and then crossed that region on land before sailing from its south coast to Tregaran, along with many other migrants. Such journeys could be perilous because of weather, piracy and highwaymen. But this good family arrived safe and well at Trepunek.

They consisted of the father and mother, Bran and Elin, with three teenage daughters, Rhian, Bethan and Mari. The family brought few possessions with them but were quite well-off financially bringing their gold and silver coins. They also had some fine clothes and other personal possessions. They could all speak some Latin, as well as the British language, and were of the Christian faith.

They were relieved but completely exhausted when they arrived. They recovered quickly with support from Owain and other residents. They soon settled into the town, taking over some abandoned farm land nearby with some small stone buildings on it. Bran was a mason by trade and was able to create a home for his family on this land and to find paid work in the building trade. After a while, he was engaged by Teged to erect a large byre at his property. As he had no son to help, Bran brought his eldest daughter, Rhian, with him to assist, by fetching and carrying things, including heavy building materials.

---

[26] Carlisle

[27] The Celtic name for Tintagel, a significant port at that time

This was when Cadwur met Rhian. He was very impressed with the young lady. Not only was she nice-looking and full of vitality but also strong enough to carry building materials to her dad. Later he discovered that she was a fine rider and enjoyed being part of the hunt. Up to that time, Cadwur had not shown much interest in the opposite sex. He was a man of action and warfare and did not have the time to think about girls. But Rhian was quite something; very feminine but also she was robust and athletic. For her part, she had never seen anyone like Cadwur. He was so strong and a brilliant horseman and hunter. She was also told of his prowess as a soldier. He thought she was wonderful and she thought he was a hero. They fell madly in love and were wed at Trepunek Church at Easter of the Year of our Lord 468. He was twenty-three and she was twenty. Rhian's family were not wealthy enough to offer a dowry having so recently migrated to Armorica. Bran agreed to undertake some more building work for Teged to help the young couple have a home of their own. In time, the couple had no less than five children who survived infancy. This was an example of how some migrants can readily integrate with the local community.

Cadwur and Bran, now his father-in-law, got on very well together. Cadwur knew little of the region from which Bran had come. Bran explained that its name in the Brythonic language was Rheged[28] and that, in terms of landscape, it was similar to the north of Cambria, with mountains and large lakes. Cadwur had heard of Hadrian's Wall. To try to demonstrate his knowledge, he explained, "When the Roman legions left Britannia and ceased defending Hadrian's Wall, the heathen Picti could just cross the Wall and invade the north and east of our country."

Bran replied, "That is partly correct, Cadwur. Terrible damage it was that these awful invaders inflicted upon our country. That much is sure. But things changed in the Gododdin[29], a home to excellent cavalry, which deterred the Picti from getting to Hadrian's Wall. The blood-thirsty Picti could not contend with a skilled and well-armed force of cavalry under expert command."

"I have heard of the Gododdin, but I am not sure of exactly where it is."

"It is the low lying part of Caledonia between Hadrian's Wall and the Antonine Wall. The latter was constructed between two main rivers in central

---

[28] Cumbria plus adjoining areas

[29] The Gododdin (Y Gododdin in British/Welsh), meaning the North, was the area between Hadrian's Wall and the Antonine Wall (which ran from the Firth of Forth to the Firth of Clyde)

Caledonia in the reign of the Emperor Antoninus Pius. There are some Picti living peacefully in the Gododdin but it is also home to powerful Celtic tribes such as the Votadini, who were allies of Rome and at times fought battles on the Roman's side, as a federate army. They are truly great horsemen.

"The Picti then ceased trying to get to and cross Hadrian's Wall and instead concentrated on invading Britannia in small boats to avoid the awesome cavalry of the Gododdin. This is how they still operate now by sea. It is difficult to apprehend them as they can strike anywhere quickly by sea and then vanish with their ill-gotten gains, which can include humans abducted a slaves. The vile and savage Scoti from the north of Hibernia operate in exactly the same way."

It then occurred to Cadwur to enquire whether the Votadini and other peoples of the Gododdin were of the Faith. He had assumed that Christianity was confined to the lands to the south of Hadrian's Wall. "Are the Votadini now Christian: I assumed not, as they live to the north of the Wall?"

Bran responded, "I am not an expert of these things and you may need to ask Joseph or Daniel. I believe that they are Christian partly through their contacts with the Romans, but also because missionaries have travelled north to tell the tribes of the Gospels. My grandfather used to speak of Bishop Ninian[30], who was a Briton and came from the west of the Gododdin. He travelled all the way to Rome, where the Pope appointed him bishop. I am told at the end of the last century, he founded a monastery called Casa Candida[31] at a location to the north and far west of Hadrian's Wall. I think my grandfather said that Ninian and some of his monks travelled deep into the lands of the Picts and converted some of them to the Faith. They say that the Picts speak a similar language to our British tongue, so that Bishop Ninian and his followers could communicate with them. I don't think he went to Dalriada, as the inhabitants there speak a different language and many of them live on remote islands or other inaccessible places."

"I have never heard of Dalriada. I don't even remember Uncle Maldwyn telling us about it."

"Again I am not an expert of such matters. My grandfather told me that there is a Kingdom of Dalriada in the north of Hibernia and that in the past peoples from that kingdom migrated to the far west of Caledonia. There they founded another part of that kingdom but owed allegiance to their king in Hibernian Dalriada. They are related to the Scoti and speak a language which they call

---

[30] This is a reference to St Ninian and accords with traditions relating to him.
[31] This monastery was situated near Whithorn, in Dumfries and Galloway

Gaelic. It seems that Bishop Ninian did not venture into Caledonian Dalriada. When we see Daniel or Joseph again, we can ask them all about Bishop Ninian."

The conversation finished with Cadwur whispering, with emotion in his voice, "There is so much to learn about the history of our homeland. I truly love Armorica which is now my home, but I should like to visit Rheged to see the mountains and lakes, and spend time in the Gododdin; to ride with those skilled Celtic horsemen. Perhaps it might happen one day."

Chapter 14
The Saint

At Trepunek, for years, people continued to grieve over the death in the year 460 of the Deacon Emyr and to be totally puzzled as to the motivation for his murder. Following a rumour which gradually spread, several people firmly believed that he was murdered by Druids or other pagans because of his position within the Christian Church. For this reason, they referred to him as a martyr, just like St Stephen, the first Christian martyr. They believed that he was deserving of the status of a saint.

Daniel, the new deacon, sympathised with these views, but, being very erudite about all ecclesiastical matters, pointed out that there was no evidence that he was murdered by non-believers because of his position as a cleric. He discounted the pile of acorns as of little or no evidential value. Daniel said that Deacon Emyr was a model Christian and indeed a murder victim; and a very sad loss to the community. But this did not of itself make him a saint as in 'the Communion of Saints' in the Christian Creed.

When Emyr's body had been buried in the cemetery, a simple headstone had been placed at the grave with an inscription, *Here lies our beloved Deacon, Emyr, who will be sorely missed by the people of this parish and all who knew him. RIP.*

Some people thought that more should be done and the idea was put forward that a cross should be placed at the location near the oak wood where he had died. This suggestion found overwhelming support and acceptance. Bran, who was a skilled carpenter, as well as a mason, constructed a magnificent holy cross in matured dark oak and it was firmly installed where Emyr had died. This took place at a ceremony which many attended and at which Daniel gave his blessing to the cross and paid his respects to his predecessor. This was a fine location on high ground with a magnificent view of the sea. It was a place to reflect on the greatness of God's creation. The people of the locality felt that this cross was a proper memorial for this devout Christian.

Some months later a lady from the town had a very young daughter who was seriously ill with a lung infection. The doctors said it was an incurable condition and there was no hope. The child was indeed very weak and had a piercing cough which was most distressing to hear. It was thought she had little time left to live.

The mother and father were at the end of their tether, partly because they had lost other children in infancy. Like many good parents they tried everything they could, including regular prayer. As a final desperate effort to save the child, they took her to Emyr's cross and there prayed to God for the child's recovery and also asked that Emyr should intercede on their behalf. They then went back home hoping against hope that their prayers would lead to a cure for the little girl.

In a few days' time, to the complete amazement of everyone, the frail little girl started to show miraculous signs of recovery. She gradually gained strength and the dreadful cough went away. With loving care and good food, she soon put on weight and became fit and well. The parents were swift to tell their friends and neighbours what had happened: people firmly believed that this was a miracle and was due to the intercession of Emyr.

When Daniel was told, he too believed that they had witnessed a miracle. He spoke of it in the church service on the following Sunday. "For people of faith, the Lord can bring healing, and miracles can happen, especially when those of faith ask for the help of a saint. A miracle is faith's dearest child. It seems that dear Emyr, a man who in his lifetime always strove to do God's will, even after death can help bring healing to this world."

Other seriously ill people were taken to Emyr's cross and were miraculously healed. The bishops at Condate were informed and readily agreed that Emyr should be looked upon as a saint. At this time in history, it seems that there was no formal procedure in the Catholic Church for canonisation and that the views and experiences of local people together with the support of the bishop of that diocese was enough to allow someone to be elevated to the Sainthood.

The belief in the miraculous powers of Emyr continued. Near to Trepunek there was a village called Plouneven[32] which was served by two springs. During a period of drought in a hot summer one of these springs dried up completely, and the other one had no more than a quarter of its usual flow. The villagers and those with farms nearby were becoming desperate, as the weather grew even

---

[32] A fictional village

hotter and there was no sign of rain on the way. A senior group of villagers visited the cross of Emyr and pleaded for his help. Later that day both springs came back to full life and there was plentiful pure water for the village and it surroundings.

The divine power of Emyr was becoming ever more established.

But still no one knew why he had been murdered or by whom.

This mystery was solved some years later in an unexpected way. The full account of this tragic death will be told at the proper time.

Chapter 15
We Need to Talk About Vortigern

In evenings when the day's work had been done, families and groups of friends liked to sit together, often around a log fire, to sing and play music but at times to talk about the state of the world. This was one of the ways in which news and information spread, sometimes at a slow pace and at times without a high degree of accuracy. Owain loved the sight and smell of a wood fire. It was something full of life and vitality, much appreciated on dark and cold winter nights. Gwen noticed that the glow of the fire would illuminate his rosy cheeks, almost as if they were glowing in the dark.

A frequent topic of conversation at Trepunek was the recent history of Britannia. This was close to the hearts of so many Britons, including those who had emigrated to Armorica. Events had thrown the lives of thousands of people into chaos and turmoil. A major issue was why the Overking of the Britons known as 'Vortigern' (in the British language as 'Guorthigern') came to enter into a pact with the Saxons allowing more of them to settle in Britannia. The Saxons were supposed to help the Britons repel the fearsome Scoti and Picti. In the event, the Saxons cooperated with the Picti to fight against the Britons. For some reason relations between the Britons and the Saxons had become sour.

In the wider world, there were a variety of opinions on the subject of Vortigern's policy but most people in Armorica were bitterly critical of this British leader and of the decisions which he took. They believed that it was a major tactical error to allow Hengist and his followers to have Tanet[33]. This gave the invaders this strategic location, with its lighthouse, which was the main gateway to Britannia for the Germanic tribes. It should have been obvious that they would spill over on to adjoining territory.

---

[33] This is the Brythonic name for the Isle of Thanet in East Kent.

Teged was exceptionally critical of him, as was his son, Cadwur, who was much influenced by his father. They called the Overking a fool and a traitor. After Vortigern had lost power in Britannia to the noble Ambrosius, there were stories circulating that he was guilty of an extravagant life-style, debauchery, incest and other vile sins of the flesh. There was even rumour that he had taken Hengist's daughter to wife. In human history such stories often follow the deposition of a ruler and are promoted by those who succeed him.

Vortigern may not have been as foolish as many thought or as debauched as those stories would suggest. He needed help against the Picti from someone, and the Romans had their work cut out elsewhere. Rightly or wrongly, he felt that the Saxons were rather more civilised than the Picti or indeed the Scoti. Some Saxons had been in Britannia for many years and many were just farmers. He thought that the British and the Saxons could live in peace together if they could defeat the Picti and the Scoti.

Uncle Maldwyn was very familiar with events in the earlier part of the fifth century, in view of his age and status in his homeland. Some events he had witnessed for himself and in other cases he was well informed from eye-witness sources. He often had much to say in these discussions, having known many of the important characters during that period. He was happy to speak at length about events in those days. In fact, he liked to speak at length about anything and everything, with even the least encouragement. Then, having listened with some degree of impatience to others, he felt that he must offer his contribution.

I met Vortigern on several occasions. He was of Celtic and Roman descent but thought of himself very much as a Briton. He was one of the British leaders in a political group established many years earlier which had actually wanted to get the Romans out, and for the Britons to take back control of their homeland. He was often heard to say, "We must take control of our own country." He discounted the value of free trade and movement within the Empire, from which Britannia would benefit. He resented Roman rule and the fact that taxes were taken and sent to Rome. He harked back to the good old times of the powerful King Cunobeline,[34] who held sway in southeast Britannia. This king, in the opinion of Vortigern, had been prudent and forceful in keeping the Romans out. Maldwyn said that Vortigern did not really see the Saxons as the serious long-term threat, which they were. He was no judge of character.

---

[34] The British King Cymbeline as in the Shakespeare play

"He seemed unaware that all Saxons were not from the same area or of the same character. He chose to enter into his pact with Hengist, who should rightly be called a Jute, as he was leader of a warrior race from a northern land called Juteland. This is a barren land where it is hard to grow crops because of poor soils and frequent storms and blizzards. One of my close friends back in Britannia had escaped from the east of the country, where he had a farmstead on good fertile land. His name was Leo and the farmstead had been in his family for generations. But on one fateful night, there was a raid by a band of heavily armed Jutes, who had arrived by sea in long rowing boats. They killed my friend's father and brother and took the women of the family into slavery. My friend had been at a neighbouring farm at the time and had no option but to escape westward to our part of the country. The nearest British militia was many miles away at Camelodunum[35]. There were several militias in this area but they were too few to cope with raids by the Jutes or other sea-borne invaders. Vortigern wrongly thought that the Jutes would be similar to those Saxons who had come to Britannia from Germania, many of whom had been driven from their land by hostile invaders from the east. Some of these Saxons came to Britannia in peace as refugees and did not pose a threat to the Britons.

"Vortigern was very wealthy and I once visited him as part of a deputation from the Cornovii at his large estate near Glevum[36], in the lovely rolling hills to the east of that city. We were treated to generous hospitality at his luxurious villa. We were pressing for a more coordinated effort by all states in Britannia to deal with the problem of the Picti and the Scoti, and to ensure that the Saxons were confined to the parts of the country allocated to them. We found Vortigern long in rhetoric but ineffective in action, particularly in getting all the leaders to work together. He was basically rather lazy and wanted a quiet and luxurious life. It is fortunate that Ambrosius, always a supporter of Rome, came to be leader of the Britons.

"I am told that Vortigern was a close friend of Bishop Agricola, who subscribed to the opinions of that loathsome theologian, Morgan. This heretic kept on preaching that men could achieve salvation by their own efforts, without the need for the Grace of God. To achieve eternal life you just needed to live what he called a good life and happy life, without feelings of guilt. He did not believe in the true doctrine of original sin, from which we were saved by the

---

[35] Colchester

[36] Gloucester

74

blood of our Lord and the Grace of God. Morgan like Vortigern was lazy and self-indulgent and thought he did not need to make a great effort to lead a pious life."

Cadwur, the son of Teged, who had studied a little theology at the abbey, was rather shocked by these remarks regarding Morgan and said, "Uncle Maldwyn, I have never even heard of Morgan. Was he a bishop and where was he from?"

"I am told that he was born in the north of Britannia. I think he was a monk and not a bishop or a presbyter: he was a windbag and a demagogue. He liked nothing better than an ill-informed crowd to preach to. His name in our British language means *Man of the Sea*. The news of his loathsome unchristian opinions spread as far as Rome and also to the great Bishop Augustine at Hippo in North Africa, who totally condemned his heretical pronouncements. At Rome he was known as Pelagius, which in Greek also means '*Man of the Sea*'. Eventually he and Vortigern fell from power. The great leader of royal descent, Ambrosius[37], who at one time had to seek refuge in Armorica, gained the status of Leader of the Britons. By then the Saxon power had grown considerably and our peoples were just beginning to be pushed back towards the west of our homeland.

"I am told that the noble Ambrosius has a son, called Ambrosius Aurelianus, who is following in his father's footsteps, in uniting the rulers of Britannia in their endeavours against the Saxons. He wants to emulate the Roman governors of Britannia, who knew how to defend the province."

Tomos the son of Owain liked hearing from Uncle Maldwyn about the history of Britannia, but was getting a little confused by the various personalities under discussion. On that day he had been working hard on the farm in the bracing fresh air, and with fatigue and lack of concentration, his eyes started to close and it was time for bed for him.

Gradually the party broke up and each member also headed for bed. Perhaps they would dream of Jutish raids and of future battles against the Saxons.

---

[37] Probably an historical figure, with a possible connection to 'King Arthur'. It is possible that there was only one Ambrosius (not a father and son).

Chapter 16
Tomos Needs a Wife

In Owain's household, he and Gwen had lost their son, Kitto, following his unfortunate battle wound. Their daughter Morwenna was happily married to Matthew and was living near Condate. They enjoyed the occasional visit from her and their grandchildren. Owain still had a farm to run and had some loyal servants to help him.

There was also their youngest, Tomos, who took over much of the responsibility for the farm and its management, something to which he was well suited. Unlike Kitto, who was amiable and liked to chat to people, and Morwenna, who was beautiful and talented in music, Tomos was what might be described as a dull man as he had no real interests outside his role as a farmer. He never went hunting or even thought of joining the militia. He had not shown any interest in the opposite sex. If he attended a carousal, he normally stood at the side and sipped cider, carefully avoiding any pressure to join in the dance. He could not play an instrument or sing. He was like his father in appearance with a round face and rosy cheeks, but did not have the broad smile or the engaging manner of his father.

He knew all about the cultivation of crops, however, and how to judge whether a cow or sheep was a good enough specimen to be acquired for the farm. His judgement in such matters was impeccable. Even when talking about farming, he said few words and his answers to questions were often monosyllabic. He was not disliked by anyone but at the same time he was not great company. One might say that he was conscientious and efficient but uninteresting.

His parents greatly valued his contribution to their world. Owain's arthritis was getting slowly but steadily worse, which limited his ability to undertake hard physical work. He regularly took herbal remedies which gave some relief but not to the extent of curing him. He even went to the cross of Emyr to ask for God's help but to no avail. Although they had good workers, Owain valued Tomos's role in supervising the farm to ensure that all was well.

In the year 469, Owain and Gwen thought that the time had come for a wife to be found for Tomos. It was well known and generally acknowledged in Armorica that every farmer who is single and over the age of twenty was in need of a wife. There were few eligible single women known to the family. Most women in the area got married quite young. Owain and Gwen were rather at a loss. Then an unexpected opportunity came their way.

One advantage of church attendance, quite apart from its spiritual significance and the enlightenment it brings, is that it is an opportunity to meet persons of the opposite sex. It so happened that a very respectable Gallo-Roman family had recently moved into the town, including an unmarried daughter of about Tomos' age. They were welcomed into the church at Trepunek, where they met Owain and his family.

The daughter's name was Emilia. She was a loyal and dutiful daughter, able to sew, spin and weave with some skill, and to carry out all kinds of housework. She helped her mother with cooking and baking. Her face and general appearance could be described as homely. She was polite but did not have very much to say for herself. The energetic Gwen, who always liked to be proactive, immediately identified her as a suitable candidate for the vacant post of Tomos' wife. Gwen became excited and optimistic at this wonderful opportunity which had fortuitously presented itself.

Back at their home, she and Owain had a discussion on this important subject and on Gwen's suggestion invited Emilia's family for supper. The invitation was gratefully accepted, and the event went very well: better even than the optimistic Gwen had expected. Both sets of parents saw the advantage of Tomos and Emilia getting together. With gentle parental encouragement over several weeks, the couple became engaged and then got married. Whatever Emilia lacked in good looks and clever conversation, she made up for in domestic skills, hard work, loyalty and efficiency. Her family offered a modest dowry of sheep and cattle, which was graciously accepted by Owain.

Eventually the couple started a family, which brought great pleasure to Owain and Gwen. Life at the farm went on happily for about ten years, with Tomos in charge, and with Owain helping as much as he could, given his age and arthritic condition. They also had farm workers and some seasonal labour.

As time went on, however, it was noticed that Gwen, who had always been so bright and focused, was getting forgetful. For example, she would start doing some cooking and wander off having forgotten about it. The food would end up burnt and inedible. She also became irate very easily over small matters, which was so unlike how she had always been. Owain became very worried about her. Emilia took over the cooking and most other domestic duties. This also tended to make Gwen ratty. Things got even worse, when it became evident that she could not remember having had a son called Kitto and having a married daughter called Morwenna. She also had a tendency to wander off into the town for no particular reason and then forget where she was and even the way home.

Owain was desperately anxious and upset, and something had to be done to help look after her. An elderly cousin, who was widowed, offered to move in with them, and take care of Gwen. This most helpful offer was accepted, but sadly Gwen's condition rapidly deteriorated and she passed away in the year 476 at the age of fifty-eight.

Owain was completely lost without her, his wife and companion over many years, including their migration to Armorica. She had so much enthusiasm and vitality, which sadly advancing age had taken away. His main comfort at this difficult time came from his elderly sheepdog, Bittou, who was at this stage no longer able to work with sheep, being too slow and hard of hearing. Owain had acquired Bittou some ten years earlier and he had been an excellent working dog, but now his days were numbered. The dog loved Owain, his good and amiable master.

Each evening when the weather was fine, Owain would take a walk from his house to a vantage point on a nearby bank to watch the sunset, taking his faithful dog with him. Both moved slowly, afflicted with the effects of old age. Then one evening, as he was seated on a rock at the usual vantage point, Owain felt a sharp pain in his chest and arm, and became short of breath. He fell to the ground in severe pain. Bittou licked his master's face and then went as fast as he could back to the house, whining and in obvious distress. Tomos came over to the dog, and guessed that the animal was trying to tell him that Owain was in trouble. Bittou led Tomos to where Owain was lying, still alive and conscious. The dog put his head on Owain's chest, whilst Tomos held his father's hand. In a few moments, Owain passed away. He was sixty years old.

The farm was left in the capable hands of Tomos and Emilia, who had both cared for Owain as best they could over the past few years. Every day on which

Tomos worked on the farm after the loss of his father, he still felt that it was his dear father's farm, of which he was only the farm manager. He felt that it was his duty to take care of it to the very best of his ability. The dog Bittou died a few days after his master.

There was great mourning for Owain and Gwen, not only within the family, but also from all the residents of the town, where Owain and his wife had been such important citizens for so many years. It was the end of an era for Trepunek.

Owain was buried beside Gwen at the cemetery at Trepunek at a service at which Daniel officiated. This was followed by a wake at the town organised by Teged and Sioned. Some excellent Roman style fare was provided for the many mourners. The cooking was carried out by two of Teged's slaves, whom he had acquired a few years previously at a high price from a noble Gaulish family in Condate. They were known to be expert in Roman culinary practice, which enhanced their price. There was a range of seafood cooked on spits over charcoal and served with the traditional Roman fish sauce, followed by wild boar served with an excellent rich sauce of herbs and spices, skilfully created by these slaves, Trevik and Minver (not their birth names but Celtic names given to them). This was followed by an array of sweet delicacies, a delight to the eye and the palate.

Teged felt that it was right and proper to lay on a fine meal following the burial of his dear brother, who had been so wise and kind in steering him to Armorica and supporting him and his family once there. Teged and Sioned grieved deeply for the loss of Owain and Gwen.

Chapter 17
The Sky at Night

In those times, the night skies were dark over Armorica: when there was no moon, the background sky could be pitch black. On a clear night, hundreds of stars were visible there. The study of the night sky was important for navigation on the seas, especially for vessels far enough away from the shore for land marks not to be visible.

Most people worked during the day and went to bed at night, but not everyone. Apart from those sentries and guards who work the night shifts, there were the astrologers.

Study of the night sky was an essential part of the lives of astrologers, who were much respected in those times, as people believed that they could predict the future from events in the night sky, including from the position of the planets in relation to the constellations and in relation to each other. A conjunction of Jupiter and Saturn, for example, was always regarded as significant and a harbinger of something.

There was an elderly and much respected astrologer who lived at Trepunek and his name was Myrddin. He had originally come from Cambria but had made his home in Armorica. When the weather was fine, he would often sleep during daylight hours and spend much of the night scanning the skies. In the Year of our Lord 451, Myrddin had seen something new in the sky just above the bright red-coloured star at the top of the constellation of Orion. It was a tiny white object and seemed to have what looked like a tail following it. He watched it for several nights and it was obvious to his seasoned eyes that it was moving against the background stars and becoming much brighter. This was truly exciting for Myrddin. He was always hoping for something out of the ordinary, such as an eclipse or a conjunction. In a few days, the object was in the constellation of Taurus and very close to the planet Mars. Very soon a few other people had observed it, and for those who did not know what it was, Myrddin explained that it was a comet.[38] These objects were regarded by astrologers as important signs of events to come. A comet near Mars, the planet of the God of War, was taken to be a sign of warfare to come, with victory for one side and defeat for the other. This still applied in the Christian era, even though Mars was a pagan deity.

This comet appeared in the month of May in the year 451 shortly before the great battle on the fields of Catalaunia when the Romans and their allies defeated Attila the Hun. In the aftermath of that battle, most astrologers were quite sure that this comet was a harbinger of the defeat of Attila. Myrddin saw the logic in that argument, but he calculated that the comet had not been moving to the south towards the location of that battle but was travelling rapidly north-eastwards towards Britannia. He feared that it was the harbinger of bad news for his countrymen in Britannia and was a sign that the Saxons would gain control of more and more of Britannia until it became a Saxon land. It might even be called 'Saxonland' or 'New Saxony' in a few years' time. He did not tell anyone else of his fears, as it would have worried them and there was little that they could do anyway to prevent the awful events which he had foreseen. The comet became fainter in a few days and then faded and disappeared.

People forgot about it, but not Myrddin, who remained fearful as to the fate of his dear homeland. His fears were gradually being realised, especially with the mass migration of Britons to Gaul in the decade beginning in the year 460.

Some devout people believed that this bright comet was just like the Star of Bethlehem as described in the Gospels, and that it was a clear sign of the second coming of Christ in the very near future. Myrddin doubted this in view of the comet's proximity to Mars on its passage across the night sky. This suggested war rather than the arrival of the Prince of Peace.

Time passed and Myrddin was getting older but still very active as an observer of the night sky. He was still blessed with very sharp eyesight. In the winter of the year 466, he was convinced that he had found a new star[39] in the constellation of Cassiopeia, one that he had never seen before, despite that fact that he observed the sky in great detail whenever there was a clear night.

---

[38] Chinese sources report a bright comet in the year 451 which is thought to be Halley's Comet

[39] This was unlikely to have been a nova or a supernova, which would have been very bright. It was probably a star previously obscured by a cloud of gas and dust which had moved away, making the star visible to the naked eye for the first time. (This episode is fictional.)

He observed this star with painstaking thoroughness over a four week period and was sure that it was not moving against the background stars. It could not therefore be a distant comet, which would be seen to move. It had to be a star. He could not contain his excitement and had to tell others of his discovery. The news spread quickly and soon came to the ears of Daniel, who was by then a presbyter, and very well versed not only in the scriptures but also in all the doctrines of the Church. He and Myrddin met after a church service and had a conversation about Myrddin's claim.

Daniel began the conversation: "I have heard it said, Myrddin, that you claim to have discovered a new star. I fear that your eyes are failing you, as new stars cannot suddenly appear. God made the heavens which are permanent and unchanging. The constellations and the fixed stars never change. There are the five moving stars which we call planets, and there are comets, but everything else is a permanent fixture."

Myrddin, who was well aware of the doctrine of the Church on these matters, was sure that this was a new star and replied with a degree of irritation, "Dear Presbyter, I assure you that my eyes are as good as they have ever been, and I know the night sky very well, especially the northern constellations which are visible throughout the year. I do not make mistakes over matters of astrology. God is almighty and, if in his infinite wisdom, he has decided to create a new star, we should accept the fact and rejoice, rather than doubting the evidence of our own eyes."

"Myrddin, what you have just said is heretical and blasphemous. As you are elderly and a respected member of our community I have no wish to report your claim to the bishop, but I would urge you to keep your opinions to yourself, as I cannot allow heresy to spread in this parish."

"I will do as you say, out of respect for you and for the Church, but I know what I have been seeing."

The two men then parted and went their separate ways, both discontented with the way the conversation had gone. Myrddin was truly amazed that a new star could come into being and, as an astrologer, pondered what its significance might be: perhaps even the second coming of the Lord. Daniel was convinced that Myrddin was mistaken and feared that, as presbyter, he would have to take the matter further, if Myrddin persisted with the heresy.

Myrddin kept his views to himself, but continued to observe this star, which he regarded as his own.

Chapter 18
Nessa the Treasure Hunter

The three children of Teged and Sioned were each very different. The eldest, Geraint, was interested in agriculture and countryside pursuits. Cadwur was a fine horseman and had aspirations to be a great warrior. The youngest, Nessa, who was just fourteen when they moved to Trepunek, was what we might call a 'tomboy': perhaps a consequence of having two brothers. She showed no interest in domestic activities expected of young women at that time, such as sewing, spinning or weaving. She was not even interested in cooking or baking, despite encouragement from her mother.

She was much closer to Cadwur than to Geraint. She was keen on horses, both riding them and just being with them. She seemed to have a natural empathy with these animals and also with other domestic animals. She too would have liked to become a cavalier and warrior, a career definitely not open to women at that time. She sometimes wondered why that was so, particularly when she was told by her parents and by Uncle Maldwyn of the campaigns of Boudicca against the might of Rome.

Nessa thought, *Boudicca was a British Celtic woman and she fought battles: I too am a British Celtic woman: why can't I do the same when the time comes?* She kept such thoughts to herself. She spent as much time as she could tending to horses at the family farm. There was a need for her services, as her father had resumed his business of horse-breeding, and was soon enjoying considerable success. Nessa was also happy to help in all the other horticultural activities of the family. This also enabled her to be out of doors. She hated to be indoors all day, whatever the season or weather.

Although Nessa did not have a beautiful voice like her cousin, Morwenna, she loved music and was learning to play the lute. She also loved to sing and dance. At times when she was in a very good mood, she would sing to the horses.

One day when Nessa was helping out with the digging in the kitchen garden, she found a few Roman coins, one of which appeared to be gold. Excited, she picked them up and ran into the house to tell her mother. They cleaned the coins and saw that some were silver and others bronze. Their markings showed that they were from the reign of the Emperor Diocletian and were therefore well over a hundred years old. When they were shown to Teged, he said that they were still valuable and used or traded at that time.

This completely unexpected find spurred Nessa on to try to find more coins. This process started in the kitchen garden. As soon as a crop was finished, Nessa was the first to offer to dig the patch over, and her offers were always accepted, as it was known that she would dig deeply hoping to find more coins or even other valuables. Sadly she did not succeed in that ambition but her intense and deep tilling of the soil was no doubt beneficial to the next crop. No one complained.

These early failures did not dampen her enthusiasm and belief that there were more things to be found somewhere in the vicinity. When she went out into the countryside with companions, she would take a trowel or small spade with her, seeking out some promising looking spot. She imagined that one day she would find a large cache of coins or valuables hidden by some rich person in the past who was never able to return to retrieve them. When not thinking about horses, Nessa's mind was on coins of gold or silver. She even dreamt of discovering such treasures.

Chapter 19
Morgan, A Suitable Case for Discussion

In the year 468, on a very special evening, Teged and Sioned had invited friends and family for a sumptuous meal at their house to celebrate Teged's fiftieth birthday. An excellent meal was being prepared by Teged's slaves, including dishes from sophisticated Roman recipes as well as some traditional Celtic fare.

The family and some of their guests arrived early. They sat in groups sipping wine and enjoying lengthy conversations. One of the groups consisted of Teged, Owain, Cadwur, Maldwyn, some folk from the town and the Presbyter Daniel.

As always, Cadwur was interested to learn about the history of Britannia and particularly the invasion of the Saxons. He had already concluded following discussions with his father that Vortigern, the Overking of the Britons, was a traitor and a fool, and also unchristian for espousing the teachings of a heretical cleric. He spoke with feeling on these matters.

Uncle Maldwyn, as always, was keen to join in any discussion. His first comments were about the heresy of Pelagianism, "We must be eternally grateful that, about forty years ago, Bishop Germanus[40] of Autissiodorum, accompanied by Bishop Lupus of Augustobona Tricassia, went to Britannia with the full approval of the Pope to combat Pelagianism and to urge its adherents to return to the true Faith. It was not just that Morgan otherwise known as Pelagius was a heretic but he and his followers led a dissolute life. Pelagius[41] liked nothing better than to bask in luxury and to be adored by his weak-minded followers. Vortigern was of the same ilk, vain and overindulgent."

---

[40] A very important historical figure. St Germans in Cornwall may have been named after him. He ordained St Patrick

[41] Again an historical figure, much denigrated by the Catholic Church

"What happened on this visit?" asked Cadwur, eager as always to learn more and not previously having heard of Bishop Germanus.

The Presbyter Daniel then joined in the conversation, speaking in his usual pious and scholarly way, "The short answer, dear Cadwur, is that the mission was successful at least for a time. Bishop Joseph gave me much information about it when we were both at Condate.

"Through the efforts of Bishops Germanus and Lupus, the British Bishops and other churchmen took heed of the counsel of the great theologian, Bishop Augustine, who had condemned the views of this dissolute man. Reliance on the Grace of our Lord is fundamental to Christianity. They urged their congregations to turn away from the heretical utterances of this imposter. Pelagius fell from favour at about the same time as the defeat of Vortigern. Unfortunately his heresy still persists in parts of the country.

"Bishop Joseph tells me that Bishop Germanus returned to Britannia on a second occasion not only to challenge the heresy but also to encourage the devout British in their struggles against the invading Saxon pagans. They say that at one battle he and his followers shouted repeatedly, 'Alleluia', which terrified the Saxons and caused then to run away."

Teged said, "That is a truly amazing story and shows the power of men of faith. Bishop Germanus must have been a very great and important man. But why was Pelagius not punished for his heresy?"

Daniel responded, "Well, as Christians we must be charitable, as Bishop Augustine has said, because we are all sinners. In time, the doctrines in those great works of Bishop Augustine will be officially declared part of the canon of the Church and thereafter anyone promoting the views of Pelagius would be a heretic. It seems that Pelagius just vanished from the scene and became a spent force. They say he died in Palestine. Perhaps in that holy land he may have seen the errors of his ways."

Cadwur, much impressed by the information about Germanus and, keen for the conversation on history and theology to continue, went on to say, "How fortunate it has been that the Romans with their huge Empire brought the true Faith to many lands including Gaul and Britannia. All the Germanic invaders of Gaul and Britannia are ignorant pagans. Christians must surely take up arms and defeat these heathens."

Joseph did not want to dampen the spirits and enthusiasm of this fine but rather bellicose young man, but he felt impelled to respond, "Dear Cadwur, there is the other path, which is to convert the heathens and let them know of the love of our Lord and the prospect of eternal life. I should add that many of the Goths were converted to Christianity a long time ago, as a result of their frequent contacts with Roman authorities and bishops. Their great Gothic religious leader, Ulfilas[42], translated the Holy Bible into the Gothic language, which was a massive task, given that there was no Gothic alphabet at the time. In about the year 340, he had to invent an alphabet and create a written Gothic language."

Teged, who had not heard of this before, said, "This is a truly remarkable story and raises the hope that in the future even the heathen Saxons and Franks might be converted to Christianity."

Daniel responded, "If it's God's will, that miracle might happen."

Daniel felt that, even though it was a birthday party and a banquet and carousal was awaited, further enlightenment in theology should be showered upon the gathering. He continued, drawing on his years of study into such matters, "I should add that the Goths did not follow the orthodox doctrines of the early Church as expounded by the influential theologian, Athenasius[43] of Alexandria, and instead followed the guidance of the Deacon Arius[44] of that same great city. They are therefore called Arians.

"The rather bitter dispute with the Arians was about the nature of God and how best to describe it. Arius did not dispute that God was in three persons: the Father, the Son and the Holy Spirit. He believed, however, that the Father came before the Son and had existed before the Son came into being, was made flesh and came to Earth. Athenasius and many others were convinced that the Father and Son were one and the same. In his view, the essence of the Faith was that God came to Earth to save mankind. God was God and the Father and Son were consubstantial; they were one and the same. God the Father did not come before God the Son. The Holy Spirit was also one and the same with them. The Holy Trinity were 'one person'. Otherwise the birth, death and resurrection of Christ made no sense in theological terms.

"The Emperor Constantine the Great was a powerful soldier and a ruler of men. The subtlety of theological debate was not something close to his heart. He had become Christian and wanted a simple understanding as to what he and all Christians should believe. He therefore called the famous Council of Nicaea in

---

[42] The information about Ulfilas is believed to be true

[43] An historical character and an important figure in early Christianity

[44] Again an important historical figure in the early church

the Year of our Lord 325, where bishops from all over Christendom gathered to settle once and for all the nature of the Holy Trinity. The arguments of Athenasius prevailed and since then we have our Christian Creed as part of the canon of the Church, which we all know and devoutly recite. This states the Father, the Son and the Holy Spirit are three persons in one and consubstantial.

"Arianism did not immediately disappear and indeed the Emperor Constantine on his death bed was baptised by an Arian Priest. One day I believe that Arianism will be rejected by all Christians, including the Goths. But it certainly cannot be said that the Goths are pagans."

Some of the group had taken in a little too much theology, important as it was. The wine had awoken their appetite, and they were eager to make a start on the festive banquet which awaited them. They hoped that Daniel would not feel the need for further elaboration regarding the goings on at Nicaea.

Fortunately, Sioned, looking festive and wearing her best gown, entered the room and could not help noticing the serious look on the faces of the men, exhibiting a mixture of interest and fatigue. Gwen followed her and encouraged them to drink again to Teged's health on his birthday, "Whatever grave matters might have been troubling you, gentlemen, it is surely now time to join in our celebration. Wonderful food and wine await you, and there will be music and dancing in the hall."

There were tempting aromas from the kitchen. The sound of stringed instruments and drums, and the lilting sound of Celtic singers were making their way from the hall. All the company made their way to the dining room.

Dancing and celebration continued into the night. The historic Council of Nicaea and its deliberations were put to one side for the rest of the evening, along with the correct way to describe the Almighty. Eating, drinking and dancing were less demanding on the human brain and spirit than theology.

Chapter 20
When Nessa Met Myrddin

Nessa continued her quest for treasure, occasionally with very limited success: a few silver or copper coins every few months, and the occasional piece of jewellery. She was one of those people who was convinced that one day she would find real success. With all the migration of people in those days into and out of Armorica, she firmly believed that there was buried treasure to be found and that she was the one to find it.

One day in the year 464 at Trepunek market, she had wandered away from her mother and happened to meet the elderly and wise Myrddin. She had spoken to him before about the stars and astrology and was most impressed with his knowledge of the night sky, a subject which she too found fascinating.

She enquired very politely whether she may ask him a question and he replied that of course she may do so. Struggling to find the right words on a subject close to her heart, she ended up asking rather bluntly, "I am looking for treasure. Where can I find it?"

Myrddin was intrigued by this question and also slightly amused by Nessa's youthful enthusiasm. He responded, "It depends on what sort of treasure you mean, young Nessa."

"Well, normal valuable treasure, like gold, silver, and jewellery. What other sort of treasure is there?"

"There are things far more precious than those you mention. Like the love which your parents have always given you, and the love you might feel for them and for your brothers. There is also the love of our Saviour.

"There are also things to be seen on a very clear night in the sky more beautiful that any jewel on Earth, like the seven stars in the group we call the Vergiliae."[45]

"I have never seen those stars; perhaps you can show them to me sometime."

"It is best to look for them as winter draws on and when Orion is prominent."

Nessa took in this information with interest and continued, "I do love my family and our Lord with all my heart, but I still yearn to find buried treasure. I do not want wealth for myself but would want to donate anything I find to my family for them to use wisely. Things found in the ground will also tell us things about the history of this beautiful land."

"That is a good answer. To find buried treasure you need to look in the right places, where people may have hidden themselves away from danger and may have lost or buried valuable objects intending to recover them later when the danger had passed."

Nessa, becoming intensely interested in his response, enquired where the right places for success might be found.

Myrddin thought for a moment, and then remembering some events from history, replied, "Well, our ancient and historical Armorican poems tell us that the blood-thirsty Julius Caesar attacked the Veneti[46] during his Gallic wars and claimed in his bombastic way to have killed them all or taken them as slaves. But he was grossly exaggerating his achievements. Powerful men often do this. We are told that many of the Veneti took to their mighty ships and sailed north to Britannia or even Hibernia. What may be significant in regard to your question is that many others of the Veneti went to Coed Arden[47] and hid themselves away until Caesar and his murderous Romans had departed to slaughter good people in other parts of Gaul. Their hiding place was this famous upland forest, a traditional place of refuge during a time of war. Others would also have taken refuge there during conflicts.

"The Veneti and others hiding away there might have lost or hidden away valuables in that remote forest."

---

[45] The Pleiades or the Seven Sisters.

[46] The Veneti were a tribe in Gaul living in the area around Vannes in what is now part of Cornouaille, Brittany. Julius Caesar claimed to have killed or enslaved them all

[47] This means 'High Forest' in early Breton and other Celtic languages and may be the origin of the expression 'Forest Of Arden'. There were a number of so called 'High Forests' in Gaul and Britain.

With excitement and exuberance, Nessa asked, "How can I get there?"

"It is many leagues from here on the west side of Armorica in the high ground to the south of the lands of Kemper[48]. You should not think of travelling alone to such a place but would need to have companions with you, and you would surely need your parents' approval. There are all sorts of danger there, including wild animals and also brigands.

"When there, you would have to think where someone would hide treasure. There would have to be some landmark which they could find in the future and which would guide them to the treasure. This might be a rocky outcrop or the border of a lake or pond or the intersection of lines from prominent objects, such as a castle or a hilltop.

"It would help you to have divining rods. But that would be difficult for you, dear Nessa, as all your family are truly devout people and divining rods are associated with paganism and witchcraft. I think they would strongly disapprove, as would Presbyter Daniel, if he ever found out that someone was using them."

"I have heard of them but aren't they used to find underground water?"

"Yes, that is their main purpose, but some people believe that they can detect metals in the ground, including gold and silver."

Nessa paused to absorb this interesting information. She dearly wanted to obtain a set of these rods, but thought it better not to say so just at that moment.

Then Sioned and Gwen came over and joined them, wondering why she was talking to Myrddin. Nessa sensed what they were thinking and said, "We were talking about the stars in the night sky. Now we are in autumn and the nights are getting longer, Myrddin says that soon we can see Orion. He was telling me how beautiful the Vergiliae are. He knows so much about astrology and it is really interesting to talk to him."

The three of them bid Myrddin goodbye and departed. Nessa was feeling excited about going to Coed Arden at some stage but kept her thoughts to herself.

---

[48] Quimper

Chapter 21
Nessa Goes to Coed Arden

During her late teenage years, Nessa continued her search for treasure, at times going a little further afield on horseback and accompanied by servants. This included trips to woods and forests, sometimes as part of a hunting trip. She found little of any value, but this did not dampen her enthusiasm. She remembered well the advice of Myrddin to go to places where people had sought refuge in days gone by.

Her big chance came in the year 467. Bishop Kaourintin[49] of Kemper had died in the year 460 and was being regarded as a saint. It was decided that there should be a pilgrimage from Domnonia to Kemper, stopping off on the return journey at various places, including the village of Kwestin[50], where the bishop had been born. This was on the boundary of the magnificent Coed Arden, the high forest famed in song and story. Nessa was more than pleased to learn that a visit to this forest was on the itinerary on the homeward journey.

Showing more enthusiasm for things ecclesiastical than expected together with a keen interest in the history of Kemper, she persuaded her parents to allow her to join the pilgrimage, along with some of her friends and three of the most trusted servants. Sioned had a rough idea that her daughter's main interest in this venture was to find places for treasure-hunting. She did not know much about Coed Arden, although she had heard the name in the past. She knew, however, that Nessa was a sensible and resourceful girl and that the trusted servants would ensure that she would avoid any trouble or danger.

---

[49] St Corentin, the first Bishop of Quimper, said to have been appointed by King Gradlon, the son of the first Overking of Armorica, Conan Meriadoc, and was consecrated by St Martin of Tours

[50] A fictional village

And so the big day came. Nessa and her friends together with her three servants joined others from Trepunek, and this whole group then combined with the party which had come from Condate. Apart from her journey from Britannia when she was little more than a child, this was the longest journey that she had ever made. The same was true of several of the young people on the pilgrimage. There was much excitement as friends met each other and pilgrims were introduced to their colleagues for the first time. Progress was slow but steady with some on horseback, some on foot and others in vehicles. There was plenty of time for people to chat as they made their way through the Armorican countryside. There was much laughter and singing as they made their way to Kemper. They camped in tents overnight, except for a few who stopped over with relatives or close friends on the way. The journey took three days.

Accommodation was arranged for them at Kemper, where they received a warm welcome. They attended divine service at the Cathedral Church, conducted by the new bishop. Nessa could not help be impressed by the city and by its fine cathedral. Everything seemed to be on a larger scale than at Trepunek, particularly the cathedral, now with its shrine to St Kaourintin. She and her fellow pilgrims were also impressed with the imposing high altar, the baptistery and the bishop's chair, with was beautifully carved in dark oak.

Nessa felt that it was a very holy place.

Kemper also had its fine rivers, along with its open spaces and ancient buildings. In the open spaces, Nessa made glances here and there wondering whether there might be scope for treasure-hunting. Apart from the autumn colours in the woods, and meadows rich with orchids and mushrooms, there was little to take her attention. In particular, there was nowhere which looked very promising for treasure-hunting and so she stored up her energy for the visit to the forest.

Much as she enjoyed being at Kemper, she could not wait for the return journey and the visit to Coed Arden, with the prospect or at least hope of finding treasure there.

The return journey took the pilgrims much further to the south to reach Kwestin and visit the shrine of the saint there. Then there was a whole day to wander through the forest. Nessa did not want to be part of a large group on this visit, and managed to form a small party with the three servants and two young women from Trepunek with whom she was very friendly.

Nessa led the way as quickly as the terrain permitted. They stopped at various places, where she and the servants at her direction dug and prodded to no avail. She did not give up hope as they walked gradually to higher ground. More unsuccessful digging took place. The servants and friends were getting just a bit fed up. Out of affection for Nessa, they did not say anything but their feelings were obvious on their faces. Nessa could not help noticing. Despite her usual optimism and determination, she thought of giving up. She consoled herself with the thought that she had visited Kemper and seen the shrine to St Kaourintin. She remembered the wise words of Myrddin that there are many types of treasure; old coins hidden in the ground were just one of them.

The group carried on walking and eventually found themselves in what seemed to be one of the highest parts of the forest. They were in a shallow glade, which was a place where they all felt a real sense of wonder. There was a strange atmosphere which they could all feel in their bones. This part of the forest had its own sounds and smells. There were strange-looking fungi and parts of old tree trunks which looked like human faces. There were loud sinister cries from groups of crows at times, as if they were trying to give the humans present some important message. A servant said that he hoped there would be no wolves about in this remote part of the forest. There was fear on some of the young faces after this remark.

Nessa was thinking again of Myrddin, and particularly about his advice on precisely where to find buried treasure. Looking around for clues she could not fail to see a massive old oak tree there, which must have been hundreds of years old. She thought, *That is the sort of feature which Myrddin had spoken of.*

She was, however, rather irritated to find a few other people arriving there. They were not part of the pilgrimage, but seemed to live in or near to the forest. They looked very relaxed and not at all hostile. On seeing them, one of her servants, who was armed with a sword, advised caution.

Then one of these folk, a handsome young man, wearing thick woollen garments, came over and, speaking in the Armoric tongue, said hello to them in a most friendly way. The young man guessed that they were treasure-hunters, as that is why visitors normally came to that part of the forest, deep inside and on high ground. He was tall and handsome with long fair hair and bright blue eyes. He continued, "If you want to find treasure these rods might help you. We have never found anything ourselves but you might be more lucky."

He then offered the rods to the servant with the sword. He was reluctant to take them, as he was sure that the young man and his companions were pagans. Nessa intervened and said, "Thank you, sir, that is a kind offer and perhaps they will bring us luck."

She bowed politely as she took the rods and then very carefully assessed the terrain. She asked herself, w*here would I bury treasure so that only I would be able to find it at a later date?* Then she noticed two other landmarks, apart from the massive oak tree: one was a tall outcrop of rock near what seemed to be the highest point of the forest and the other was the ruin of an old stone building high up on a ridge. In her mind, Nessa imagined lines joining these three points, which she estimated to form a perfect equilateral triangle. In a flash of inspiration she decided to identify the centre of this triangle, which turned out to be an area of soft and damp ground near the edge of a large pond. Some moorhens swam away as Nessa stepped over reeds to get to the spot she had selected, following her engagement with geometry.

She directed her long-suffering servants to go to that place with their spades and trowels. Nessa held the rods over several spots and, after about half an hour, felt a sudden and strong tingling sensation in her arms. Feeling both shocked and excited, she put down the rods and, having begun to dig at that spot, found that the ground was like peat. After hard work for another half hour, Nessa hit something hard. Her servants moved over to help and they pulled out a small metal case. They wiped it as best they could and were able to open it. To their amazement, it was full of gold and silver coins, sparkling clean as if they had just been minted. Nessa could not believe her eyes.

Her servants and friends were equally amazed, as was the young man who had given her the rods and his companions. She was shaking with excitement. This is what she had dreamt of. The young man who had given her the rods and who was looking on, shouted, "Well done, gentle lady. You must have magical powers."

Nessa knew he meant well and it was just a throwaway remark but even so she had a guilty feeling that she was engaging in the forbidden arts. But at the same time, she felt strongly that she was using a scientific method by identifying a place where someone might choose to hide treasure. She carried on with the rods, hoping to find more treasure.

But Nessa found more than she had bargained for, as suddenly the rods started to move violently in her hands. Feeling shocked and terrified, she had to put them down. She asked the servants to stand back as she herself did some more careful digging next to the place where the metal case had been found. There was no more treasure but to her horror she found firstly a human skull and then discovered that it was part of a whole skeleton. Nessa was close to fainting and her servants rushed over to hold on to her. She tried to say something, but the words would just not come out. There was absolute silence for a few moments.

Then suddenly, a tall handsome man appeared out of nowhere. He was dressed in a long pure white robe. He had long dark brown hair and a matching long beard. He wore rope sandals on his elegant feet.

He had the most beautiful brown eyes and a benign and saintly expression on his handsome face. Nessa looked at him but had to avert her eyes immediately, as she was convinced that it was the Lord Jesus Christ. She and those present fell to the ground, as if in worship. Someone whispered, "It is the Lord."

Then the man spoke in a Brythonic dialect, which Nessa and some of her companions were just about able to understand. He had a deep and authoritative voice, "Fear not, young people. I am not the Lord Jesus Christ, but I am from the spirit world. My name is Garomaros and I was of the Veneti people, who were attacked by the Romans at the time of Gaius Julius Caesar. I was wounded in a fierce battle and my comrades brought me here with them, when they took refuge in this forest. We had fought bravely, but the Romans had better weapons and more warriors than on our side, and so we had to accept a humiliating defeat.

"My wounds were severe, and I died here in pain and sorrow. My comrades buried me where you found my remains. They buried my coins with me, as at that time we believed that the dead would need money to get to the next world. You have just discovered my earthly remains, which have been lost for over four hundred years. My comrades, who had brought me here, departed when it was safe for them to leave. They thought that I was safely at rest, after a duly dignified burial in accordance with their pagan traditions.

"I was not, however, able to rest and my spirit has wandered around Armorica ever since that time. Then I met the blessed St Anne[51], the mother of the Virgin Mary, and she told me of the birth, life, death and resurrection of our Saviour. I became a believer but did not feel able to go to the next world until my remains had received a Christian burial, rather than a mere pagan one.

---

[51] St Anne, who was believed to be the mother of the Virgin Mary, is the Patron Saint of Brittany.

"Young people, if you are true Christians as you seem to be, please exhume my remains and take them to the village near here for burial at its burial place. The coins you may take, as there is no fee in money for entering the Kingdom of Heaven.

"Use this money for righteous purposes."

Nessa, who was shocked to her core, found from somewhere the strength to stand and say in a faltering voice, "I promise you, sir, that we will do exactly what you have asked. Your earthly remains shall have a Christian burial and I will give the coins to my beloved parents, who are devout Christians and will apply them to righteous purposes."

"I thank you, good lady, with all my heart."

Then Garomaros vanished as suddenly as he had appeared and was never seen again. They all fervently hoped that he would find his way to the Kingdom of Heaven.

The group who resided in the forest (including the young man who had spoken with Nessa) were also shaken to the core by this apparition. They had previously heard of the Christian Gospels but now were converted from paganism to the Faith. They were all baptised a few days later. They had taken back their divining rods at the scene and thrown them away into the nearby pond. Nessa saw them doing this.

Nessa and her company made a timber stretcher and carefully and respectfully placed upon it the remains, covered in a woollen blanket, to take it to the local place of burial. They told the amazing story of Garomaros to the presbyter at Kwestin, who later that day conducted a burial at the cemetery in full accordance with the liturgy of the Catholic Church. He also prayed for the soul of this remarkable man and gave a blessing to Nessa and her group.

This event was a pivotal moment in the life of Nessa. Few people in the world could ever have had such an experience. Everyone there was also similarly moved and affected.

Chapter 22
Nessa Contemplates Her Future

When she had returned home, Nessa told her parents the story of her fantastic time in Coed Arden. She spoke in a very modest and respectful way, giving all the details of what she had done and the results of her activity. She omitted to mention the divining rods, as she was sure that mention of them would have introduce a discordant element into the conversation. Her voice trembled as she spoke of Garomaros. When she had finished her account of this fantastic event, she felt drained, but relieved at the same time, having shared her experiences with her parents.

She dutifully handed over the coins to her father, as she had promised to Garamoros. Teged was truly amazed by the whole story and promised faithfully to use this money for righteous purposes. Sioned went down on her knees to pray. In her heart, she wished she had been there and witnessed the stunning event.

When she had risen, Teged and those around him composed themselves and without delay went to visit the Presbyter Daniel to ask for prayers in the church. Daniel was very moved by the account of what had happened. He prayed for the family and for the soul of the man who had appeared in the forest. He added that miracles can still happen and that one day the Lord Jesus Christ will appear and walk amongst us. He said that we now know that the blessed St Anne is abroad in our land. He said that was a sure sign that God will safeguard our community and the whole of Armorica.

A few days later and after he had given the matter much thought, Teged discussed his ideas for the money with his wife and children.

"One wish I have had ever since we moved to Armorica was to make a pilgrimage to Rome and, if I could be permitted, to have an audience with the Holy Father.

"This is something I feel impelled to do before I die; and I am now no longer a young man and in time will need to hand over our estate to the next generation. I would wish to make this journey when I am retired from my daily chores and duties. If you agree, I should like to put aside a small part of this money for that purpose, as a pilgrimage as long as that would involve considerable expense.

"I think that all the remainder of the money should be donated to the abbey at Ponterle to say prayers for the soul of the truly remarkable man to whom the money belonged and who was converted to the Faith.

"The abbot would ensure that the money would be well spent on the good works of the abbey and that Garomaros would always be remembered in their prayers."

There was silence whilst everyone considered what Teged had said.

Nessa was in tears and Sioned comforted her and asked her why she was so upset. "Did you find the whole episode in the forest very distressing?"

Nessa wiped away her tears and responded, "It was partly that but mainly the thought that one day Dad is going to die. I love you both and don't think I could live without you."

Teged took her in his arms and said very tenderly, "Everyone is going to die at some stage. In the meantime we must live an active and full life, always remembering our duties as Christians. Through the Grace of God and the sacrifice of our Saviour, we are promised eternal life. There is no need for fear or sadness. If it's God's will, I shall be with you for many more years. Long enough to visit Rome and much more."

The others shared Nessa's feelings, but did not show their emotions in such an obvious way.

All of them whole-heartedly agreed with Teged's wishes for the use of the money. Later that year, he delivered the main part of the money to the abbey for the intended purposes, including the request for regular prayers for Garamoros. It was most gratefully and graciously received by the abbot, who was inspired when he heard the story of how the money was found, particularly the reference to St Anne, the Patron Saint of Armorica, and the conversion of a lost soul to the Faith.

The abbot said in a serene voice, "To think that the blessed St Anne has been abroad in our lands and has converted the troubled soul of this man to the true Faith."

Over the coming weeks, Teged and Sioned noticed a change in Nessa after these events. She ceased to be so headstrong and self-assured, and became more reflective and empathetic with others. She retained her love of and feelings for horses and other animals, which, if anything, became even stronger. She no longer showed any desire to search for treasure. She needed to think long and hard about how she wanted to spend her life.

Her mood seemed to change from day to day. Some days she felt that she would like in some way to aid the militia of which her brother, Cadwur, was a member. If they would not let her join in combat, she could surely groom and prepare some of their horses for training sessions or indeed for battle. Unfortunately, Cadwur was very dismissive of this idea when she approached him about it. He felt strongly that the militia and the circumstances in which it operated were no place for a woman. He recognised that his sister was physically strong and also mentally made of stern stuff, but he felt that women could not cope with the pressures of war even as helpers rather than combatants. It seems that he had forgotten all about the warlike Boudicca.

Some days Nessa wondered about leading a purely religious life. She pondered whether the apparition which she had seen was some sort of sign that she should enter a monastery. One day Uncle Maldwyn saw her sitting outside the stables, where she had been mucking out. As she looked very pensive, he asked her whether she was alright.

"Yes, Uncle Maldwyn, I am fine but I was thinking how I could lead a more religious life. Are there such things as monasteries for women? Can women become monks?"

"I am told that there is an abbey near Naoned where women are allowed to enter and live, to carry out domestic duties, and are required to devote themselves to prayer. They have their own wing where they live and do not mix with the monks. They have to swear an oath of chastity and an oath to remain at the abbey."

"I will think about that, as at least I would be serving the Lord."

The idea did not really appeal to her, as she thought there should be religious institutions specifically for women with a woman in charge. Neither she nor Maldwyn knew of any such places.[52]

---

[52] St Bridget is said to have established an abbey for nuns in Ireland in about 480, but there may not have been any such places in Armorica in that century.

Whilst Nessa was contemplating how she might wish to spend the rest of her life, she continued to care for the horses and also tend to other animals.

She sometimes wondered whether horses had souls and whether there were any of these animals in the Kingdom of Heaven. She knew that Jesus had ridden on a donkey, but it seemed he may never have ridden on a horse. He was, however, born in a stable where there were farm animals and perhaps he was a lover of animals. It is fair to say that according to the Gospels he was not a lover of swine—a domestic animal commonly found in the Roman world.

One thing that was never on Nessa's mind was marriage and having a family.

It was not that she did not like men. It was also the case that she was not sexually attracted to other women. Marriage to her meant being indoors and doing domestic chores, which she found boring. She willingly helped her mother when necessary, but they were in the happy position of having domestic servants as well as slaves so that she could normally spend her time out of doors. She had no thoughts about having children. Bringing horses into the world was quite enough excitement and fulfilment for her.

Chapter 23
Down on the Farm

In the year 472, there was much action by the militias in view of constant threats from the Franks in the east and the Visigoths to the south. Cadwur and Matthew again excelled in battles and became commanders of cavalry squadrons. Many other young men joined militias, with the encouragement of the local rulers. Wages for the warriors were increased, as were taxes on the landowners, including Owain and Teged. The other consequence of the military situation was that there was a shortage of agricultural workers, as some men left the land temporarily for better wages in a militia. Owain and Tomos were badly affected by this trend, as the harvest was not far off and they were short of their usual casual labourers.

In this troubled context, Tomos was rather pleased to have a visit from two young men who said they were brothers who were looking for work. They were both tall and looked very fit and healthy, and one of them spoke to Tomos, in an Armoric dialect which he just about understood, "My name is Medar and this is my younger brother Pereg. We are looking for work, as we have been crewing in fishing boats near Tregaran. Unfortunately the large trawler on which we were working ran aground in some rough weather and was severely damaged. The skipper says he will have to wait for the next large spring tide to try to get it afloat and then it will be out of action for weeks whilst it is repaired. We were lucky to escape. The captain let the crew go on the lifeboats but he bravely remained on board. We hope he will be safe there on his own. We were, however, laid off and currently have no income and so we wonder if there is any help you need on your farm.

"Pereg and I were brought up on a farm in the south of Armorica. Our family had to give up the farm when our father was killed in a battle against the warlike Visigoths, who took our land. So we took up work in the boats. On our way here we called at the church and met the helpful presbyter, who suggested that we visit you and offer our services."

Tomos, who was a man of few words but with sound judgement about animals and also about people, was impressed with these young men.

In his usual blunt way, he asked, "Are you Christians? Do you go to church every Sunday? Can you use a scythe? Can you plough with oxen or heavy horses? Can you weed a field of swedes and cabbages?"

Medar was in turn impressed with Tomos, a man who did not waste words and got to the point. He replied in a positive and amicable way, "Yes, sir, to all your questions. We were brought up in the old religion, but have been converted to the true religion and have been baptised. We are devout Christians. We can do all the types of work you mention. We do not enjoy weeding but know it has to be done and take pride in a field free of weeds.

"We can also groom and exercise horses, and milk cows. Pereg is excellent at shearing sheep. We are well used to dealing with lambing. We are looking for a fair wage and lodgings but no more than that."

Tomos nodded with approval and said he would ask his father to come and join them. Then Owain came over with his old friend and steward, Ifor, to meet the new arrivals. A few words were exchanged. Owain, who tended to like everyone, was impressed by the young visitors. The acid test was the hard-headed and sceptical Ifor, who looked the visitors over and paid attention to what they had to say. He too thought that the young men were genuine and that they should be hired. He nodded his approval to Owain: high commendation indeed.

A fair wage was agreed and they were shown to a vacant bothie, as to serve as their accommodation. Medar and Pereg began work. They proved to be as good as their word. Not only did they work hard and efficiently but they were always polite and courteous to Owain and his family. Owain thought that perhaps God had sent them knowing that he was short of help on his farm. He had never seen the fields so clear of weeds or the wheat, oats and barley so skilfully harvested. In late September, however, the young men received word that the fishing boat had been re-floated and repaired and that the skipper would like them to return as soon as possible.

On the Sunday before they were due to depart, they attended church with Owain's family. This was also an occasion when Teged and his family, with the exception of Cadwur, who was away with the militia, also attended for the Eucharist. As the congregation were leaving, Nessa saw Medar and Pereg and, for her, time stood still. She and Medar could not take their eyes off each other. The others present were rather puzzled.

The reason for her extreme reaction was that Medar was, without doubt, the young man who had given her the divining rods in Coed Arden that eventful day, when they had both witnessed the fantastic apparition. On that occasion she saw how generous and polite he was; not at all envious of the fact that she had found treasure when he had never been able to do so. She saw how moved he was by the spirit of Garamoros and what he had to say. She noticed that the young man had thrown away the divining rods, apparently in a gesture against paganism. She had also noticed in the forest how handsome he was. She also recognised Pereg as one of the group of companions at that scene.

Medar for his part had been very impressed by Nessa at that scene, not only by her obvious skill in searching out treasure, but her composure faced with the trauma of finding human remains and then being confronted by a being from the spirit world. The way she responded to the spiritual being showed maturity and grace at a level which he did not imagine any young person could have attained. He would have been lost for words, but she had managed to respond in a dignified and moving way.

It became apparent to the others present outside the church that the two young people knew each other. An explanation was needed and so Nessa then in a spirit of amazement and excitement addressed them, "This gentleman, whom I now know to be called Medar, was present at Coed Arden when the apparition came before us. He and his friends were as affected as we were by this awesome event."

"That is quite true," said Medar, "until then, we had followed our family in the religion of the pagans, but the words spoken by that troubled man from the spirit world and his references to St Anne and to our Saviour totally changed our lives. My brother and I and others from our group were converted to the Christian religion and were baptised at the little church in the village of Kwestin. Since then the lives of my brother and myself have been transformed. Our days are filled with gladness and devotion to all our duties both temporal and eternal. The young lady who now recognises us, and whose name we still do not know, behaved with great courage and dignity at that astonishing occasion."

Nessa responded, "Medar, my name is Nessa and I am the niece of Owain and the cousin of Tomos."

Owain with a benign smile on his round face thought, *These men really have been sent by God to assist us in our time of need.*

That evening, both families had their supper together, with the rest of Owain's household and with Medar and Pereg also present. After the meal, Nessa met up with Medar and urged him to stay a little longer at Trepunek. Sioned could not help noticing the way her daughter was looking at Medar. There was a look of affection and tenderness in her eyes, which Sioned had never seen before when Nessa was in the company of a young man. Occasionally she might have that sort of expression but only when caring for a young colt or filly.

Medar agreed to stay longer, whilst Pereg decided to go back to the skipper to help with the boat. After his day's work for Owain and Tomos, Medar spent some time with Nessa at Teged's estate, both working, riding horses and playing music together. They might have fallen in love anyway, but their joint experience in the forest was an unbreakable bond between them. A few weeks later, Medar asked Teged for Nessa's hand and he and his wife were glad to consent. Teged raised the question of a dowry. Medar replied that he would like to reside on the estate with Nessa and make it their home and that there was no need for a dowry. Sioned was particularly pleased for her daughter, as she did not like the idea of a military or a monastic life for Nessa. As for Nessa, any thought of those careers evaporated. Having found the right man, even the idea of domestic duties did now not seem so very bad.

Chapter 24
St Briog Comes to Domnonia

In the Year of our Lord 480, another monastery was founded in Domnonia at a location near its north coast to the west of Condate. A British monk called Briog[53] from a part of Cambria known as Ceredigion was its founder. He had been baptised as a Christian in his home country, and had later studied theology in Hibernia. After he had migrated to Gaul, he visited Bishop Germanus at Autissiodorum and gained much insight into the paths of righteousness from this great pillar of the Church. Germanus, appreciating that Briog was fluent in the Brythonic tongue, as well as in Latin, advised him to relocate to Armorica to found a monastery there, to complement the abbey at Ponterle. Germanus knew the Abbot Clement at that abbey and was sure that he would be only too happy to assist Briog. Germanus felt that Briog with his fluency in Brythonic would greatly help those migrants from Britannia who spoke little Latin, mainly those from the poorer classes.

Briog visited the bishops at and near Condate and received financial help from them and from other sources. And so the new monastery came into being.

Bishop Joseph invited his friend Teged to join him in a visit to the site where the new monastery was under construction. They met Briog there and Teged was struck by his piety, his determination and the sheer force of his personality. Briog told them of his time with Bishop Germanus, but also about his time of study and reflection at a monastery in the land of Hibernia. They were fascinated to know that the Christian Faith had spread to a land hitherto thought of as barbaric

---

[53] Briog (or Brioc in the Armorican dialect) was a historical character and one of the founding saints of Brittany. He gave his name to the town of St Brieuc, near where his monastery was founded. It is believed that he was guided by St Germanus, but not known precisely what advice he received.

and uncivilised, which the Romans had called the land of winter, where all sorts of monsters were believed to wander about.

Joseph and Teged returned to their respective homes, pleased to know that the Faith was becoming ever more established in Armorica.

Chapter 25
The Last Words of a Blacksmith

Lukaz was a blacksmith in Langaron[54], a coastal town situated to the south of Kemper. He had performed that role in the town for about twenty years with skill and devotion and was by now elderly and no longer in robust health.

He had come there as a refugee and found work at the smithy, then operated by a local man called Aaron. Lukaz had worked hard and well and was able to take over the business when Aaron retired. Lukaz had never married and kept himself to himself. He never spoke to anyone about his earlier life, and the local people assumed that perhaps unpleasant things might have happened to him and whatever family he might have had. Apart from making and fitting horseshoes, as was usual in those days, Lukaz made a whole range of metal objects, such as fire-irons, swords, spears and spits.

He was much respected as a craftsman. He had an assistant called Konzelveg, whom he had trained well and who was able to do much of the work. They called him 'Kon' for short. Kon was a strong as an ox and well suited to life as a blacksmith.

In the year 482, Lukaz's health had been deteriorating for a while. He lacked energy and was at times short of breath. One day at the forge, he collapsed and was hardly able to breathe. He sensed that he did not have long to live. Kon came over to him, put a support under his head, and gave him some water to drink. Lukaz quickly came to himself and asked Kon to go and ask the local presbyter to come, as he wished to make his confession. Kon was reluctant to leave him but did what he was asked to do. On leaving, he asked a neighbour and friend to stay with Lukaz whilst he went on his distressing errand.

---

[54] A fictional town

When the presbyter arrived, forewarned and looking anxious, he and Lukaz went together into the back room, whilst Kon attended to the smithy.

The presbyter, who saw that Lukaz was ill and troubled, invited him to make his confession.

"Thank you for coming. I feel that I am not long for this world and want to find peace before I depart. There is a long story, which needs to be told.

"I was born and brought up in eastern Gaul, which at the time was in turmoil with so many invaders from different tribes. We did not know what would happen and our people had to fend for themselves. I got into bad company and joined a gang of criminals who looted and stole particularly from those escaping from invaders. My name was then Lucius, which I changed to Lukaz, when I renewed my Christian vows in this region.

"When we had obtained a large amount of money and valuables, the five of us in the gang decided to relocate to Armorica to set up a new life in a safer part of the world and where no one would know of our background or our criminal activities. We were, however, cheated by the leader of the gang, who in the dead of night stole all the money and valuables and raced away on his swift horse. This happened near Condate. Two of the gang had become ill and went back into the lands controlled by the Franks. I and another gang member decided to track down the leader and make him pay for what he had done.

"This awful man was called Claudius and after days of investigation we discovered that he had been in the area of Trepunek. We hid away in an oak wood near there and hoped that he might come past, carrying the two leather bags in which the loot would be contained. We had almost given up and it was by now almost dusk.

"We then saw what we thought was Claudius lying apparently asleep near the wood in a shady spot. We were sure that our luck was in and that we had been rewarded for our pertinacity. The man we saw in the fading light looked just like Claudius and had two leather bags very close to him.

"I was filled with an irresistible rage hotter than my fire in the smithy out there. I thought that Claudius would be armed and that we had to act first, as he was a much better swordsman than either of us.

"And so we sprang on him and filled with rage I stabbed him through the heart with my razor-sharp sword.

"As he was dying, the man asked for God's mercy. I knew immediately that it was not Claudius' voice, both from the tone of it, from his accent and from the plea to God.

"We took the bags and found no money or valuables but just basic food and drink and also communion bread and wine.

"I was devastated with grief and guilt. We found some acorns and laid them on his dead body in a pile. We knew that this was a Druidic symbol, which might draw suspicion from us if we were ever found. It all happened so quickly and then we heard the sound of a flock of sheep approaching, and the barking of a sheepdog. Totally shocked and in turmoil, we left the bags and rushed deep into the wood, where we hid until the coast was clear.

"I have since learnt that the man we killed was the Deacon of Trepunek, Emyr, who is now a saint. I do not want to go into the next world without confessing this terrible crime and begging for God's forgiveness. To kill any human is a sin and contrary to the Ten Commandments but to kill a saint is an abomination, for which I feel heartily ashamed. I pray that the Good Lord will judge me with mercy."

Lukaz then stopped speaking, and tears filled his eyes. He was very short of breath and knew he was soon to die.

The presbyter was very distressed and moved by this story. He was momentarily lost for words. Then Lukaz spoke again:

"Father, please go to Trepunek for me and tell the presbyter there just how the tragic death of St Emyr came about. The good people there need to know."

Lukaz then unlocked and opened a drawer and took out a bag of coins which he handed to his confessor.

"This is my worldly wealth, except for the smithy itself, which I want Konzelveg to have. Please take this money and give it to the Presbyter of Trepunek to use for the purposes of that parish."

The confessor said, "I will do what you have asked and I will pray to God for absolution for your sins through his Grace."

Lukaz no longer had anything to live for and passed away peacefully in the presence of his confessor, who performed the last rites.

Lukaz's companion at the time of the murder had parted from him and made his own way in the world. He had drowned at sea a few years earlier during a storm whilst employed as a fisherman.

No one knew what had become of the dreadful Claudius.

He had in fact relocated to Naoned and lived the rest of his days in comfort not far short of luxury. No one there ever found out his true identity or the source of his wealth. His story to Owain about his father dying of apoplexy following a raid by the Alani was a cynical pack of lies. Claudius would never have been found lying on the highway verge near to Tregaran, had his horse not broken a leg. He left it to die and later, after his stay at Trepunek, stole another horse on his way south, which took him to his final destination. When he thought about Owain and Gwen, his only sentiment was not gratitude but "just how gullible can people be." When found on the verge, he would have been armed, but, as he fell to the ground beside the highway, he held on to his bags so firmly that he dropped his heavy sword, which slipped down into a deep ditch and out of his reach.

When the news of Lukaz's confession reached Trepunek, there was a mixture of deeply felt emotions. Mainly it was a relief to know precisely why Emyr had been murdered, and that it was not an attack on his religion by Druids or other pagans, but a tragic case of mistaken identity. There was some small sympathy for Lukaz, as at least he had shown great remorse and owned up to his sins. The anger with Claudius was something the whole community felt: his treachery, his lies, his life of crime. No one in the town knew where he was at that time, and that he was enjoying the fruits of his crimes. There was sadness too that Owain and Gwen never got to learn how Emyr came to be murdered.

Chapter 26
The Adventures of Young Kitto

In the same year as Lukaz's confession and death, Cadwur and Rhian were now parents with a growing family of four children, the youngest being Kitto, who was twelve and named after Cadwur's cousin, who had sadly died as a result of a wound in battle. Young Kitto was attending the abbey to study there, but in his heart preferred physical activities to learning about Latin grammar. He was studying that language as written by the classical authors, such as Cicero and Julius Caesar, but he was well aware that the Latin now spoken by everyone was rather different. In over four hundred years, the language was slowly evolving into what eventually became French. He knew that he needed to learn Latin for various reasons including to be able to read the Vulgate Bible. He found the other subjects rather more interesting, especially astrology, which had practical uses such as for navigation. He was very conscientious, however, in all his studies, including that of the Latin language, which he could speak and write very well. Cadwur was impressed with this, as soon Kitto was rather better at reading and writing Latin than he was.

Kitto was like his father in looks and attitudes. He loved sporting activities including archery, hunting, fishing and horse-riding. He looked forward to the day when he might join a militia. His father was his role-model and his hero. He too wanted to be a warrior. Whenever he could he loved to practice firing arrows at a target, trying all the time to get more accurate. His father had given him a javelin and he also loved to practice throwing it as far and as accurately as possible. It was one with a specially hardened iron tip, so that it could be thrown many times without degrading. Some of the javelins used by the militias had softer iron tips and were intended for single use.

His older siblings were all girls, whom he found rather irritating. He would have preferred a brother, with whom he could have gone off on adventures. One or other of his sisters was often complaining about something he had done, and at times accusing him of causing some problem. In most cases, they probably had some good reason to complain about him. He was good friends with Matthew's son, Luke, who was about the same age and who lived near Condate. They used to visit each other regularly. Young Luke was named after the cousin of his father, who had been a monk but had died. Both boys therefore bore the name of a deceased relative and in a way felt the same sense of responsibility to honour their deceased family member. Luke also had one of the javelins with a hardened tip.

The two boys loved archery and would compete to see who could get the most bullseyes. They were also both skilled with throwing javelins. They practised together for distance and accuracy and achieved high standards for their age, both with javelins and in archery. With javelins, they would practice for hours at targets at various distances from them. They did not allow themselves a throw at a more distant target until they had hit the nearer one three times. Kitto was able to throw accurately for up to fifty yards, quite an achievement for a boy of his age. His friend was not quite so good but still performed creditably.

One of their pleasures was to go off on their own for long walks in the various woods near Condate. They did not take javelins with them on these walks, but sometimes did some archery as they went along. They were usually back at Matthew's house by early evening, but one day there will still not home when it was getting dark. Morwenna, Luke's mother, was getting worried and went out to the fields to tell her husband Matthew that they were still not home.

Matthew was not too worried. "Perhaps they had lost track of time or maybe taken a wrong turn. You know what boys are like."

They did not return that night and next morning Matthew and a servant saddled up their horses and rode out to the woods to look for them. He was by now very worried. The two riders went along all the tracks in the woods but found nothing, no sign of the boys or any indication of where they might have gone.

They did not give up and, after following these routes for a second time, they found a boy's coat of the type which Kitto wore, but there was no sign of the boys. There were, however, in that location a lot of hoof and foot prints, and some piles of horse droppings. They then found a quiver, which looked like the one belonging to Luke. Matthew was beginning to fear that they might have been abducted.

Matthew rode back at great speed to Condate and alerted the commander of the militia. He composed himself but spoke almost breathlessly and showing his obvious anxiety.

"My son, Luke, who is just twelve, has gone missing in the woods along with his friend, Kitto, who is the same age. It is not like them to stay away like this. They are very reliable and had no reason in the world to want to run away from home. I found a coat and a quiver which belonged to them. I dread to think what might have happened to them."

The commander, Lucullus, replied in sombre tones, "It is possible that they have been abducted. There have been reports from the lands under control of the Franks of criminal gangs abducting children for sale into slavery, particularly to the Alemanni. The Franks have cracked down on them and maybe they are moving into our territory. I will immediately get a party together to search the area. You must join us, Matthew."

The party of eight riders set off for the woods and split into sets of two to cover as much ground as possible. They were to meet up at the 'bent oak field gate' in two hours' time to compare notes.

It was getting close to the end of the two hours when suddenly a boy was seen riding a horse in the general direction of Condate. He was recognised as Kitto, the son of Cadwur. The two members of the militia caught up with him. He was in a dishevelled state and looked as if he might have been injured. He could barely hold on to the horse.

"Kitto, whatever has happened?"

Breathlessly, the boy answered, "We were captured in the woods by some men, who tied us up and took us to that old building on the hill up there. I managed to escape. Some of them had left just now and there was one left behind to guard us. I think he might have been drunk as he did not notice that I managed to cut my ropes with a small knife which I carry with me. When I was free he jumped at me, but I managed to tip a heavy table on to him and I was able to run away. There was a horse outside which I mounted and rode here, bareback. Luke is still there and is in great danger. I left him as I thought it was better to get away and ask for help."

"You did the right thing and are a brave lad."

Then fortuitously two other members of the militia, hearing the noise, arrived. One of them took Kitto back to Matthew's family estate and the other three rode swiftly to the building which Kitto had pointed out. There they found

114

Luke gagged and tied up: and a man, his guard, lying on the ground apparently semi-conscious.

They untied and released Luke, who was very distressed, but seemed to be uninjured. As they were about to leave, they saw three men on horseback riding towards the building. Two of them were holding young girls on their horses.

These riders dismounted and took the terrified young girls into the building, only to find that their other captives were not there and that their colleague was lying motionless on the floor. That was not the only surprise for them; they were immediately confronted by three armed militiamen, who easily overpowered them and released the girls. A militiaman called Pol, who was a battle-hardened warrior, had his foot on the chest of one of the villains and his sword point on his throat. The other two had already been tied and bound by the other militiamen.

Pol asked the villain, "Who are you and where are you from?"

The man answered in Latin, terrified and hardly able to speak, "We are Gauls who lived near Lutetia[55]. The Franks took our land and we fled, finding it hard to make a living. Agents of the Alemanni offered us good money if we could find slaves for them." Then he stopped. He could say no more, but he had already said enough.

The villains were taken to Condate where they were later put in trial by the ruler of the district. They were sentenced to death for their vile crimes.

The two girls had been returned to their families and Kitto and Luke went to their respective homes. There was much relief that they had been saved but, thereafter, they were not allowed to venture on long walks on their own in the area of Condate. Kitto was not too pleased, as he had a sword which he could take with him, and which he knew how to use. Luke was less bold and appreciated an armed adult with him when he went out into the woods.

Kitto also constantly begged his father to allow him to train with the militia, although the age limit for this was fourteen. At last Cadwur gave in to him and he was allowed to join in. His skills as a rider, swordsman, a javelin thrower and an archer increased dramatically. It was obvious that he had the making of a warrior.

---

[55] Roman name for Paris

Chapter 27
Teged's Journey

The abduction and rescue of Kitto and his friend in the year 482 had a profound effect on the family, especially on Teged, who had now retired from his career as a horse-breeder and trader, and from the management of his estate. Nessa with her husband Medar had effectively taken over the equine business and Geraint was gradually taking over as manager of the estate and the farming business. Cadwur gave support, but was often away with the militia.

Teged was now planning for his pilgrimage to the Holy City. He was feeling an acute sense of guilt at having kept slaves, partly from religious convictions and also from the prospect of meeting the Pope. More than anything he thought of his own grandson, Kitto, who was very close to ending up in slavery. After thoughtful discussion with Sioned and his children, he decided to grant their freedom to his slaves.

These included his expert cooks, who were delighted at the prospect of spending the rest of their lives as freemen. Teged spoke to them, "You have served me well and loyally for years. You are now free to do whatever you wish. I should be pleased if you would stay with us and work as before but as servants for fair wages. But if you want to move away, that is now your right."

Trevik responded on behalf of them, "You have always treated us fairly, master, and with respect, and we should like to remain with you as your servants. Minver and I also have dreamt of setting up in business, and, on the days when we might not be needed here, to offer catering services to other families for special events."

Teged was a little taken aback but also impressed by their ambition. He said.

"That sounds like an admirable plan and, if I can help by putting in a good word for you, I will be pleased to do that. You are both very skilled in the art of cuisine and people would surely want to use your services."

In the following days, Teged had long discussions with Joseph at Condate, where he was now a bishop, about a possible pilgrimage to Rome. He had discovered that Joseph too had the pious hope of making a pilgrimage to Rome. Eventually and after further talks with several members of the clergy and with laymen, a group of twelve pilgrims, including Bishop Joseph and Teged, was formed.

Consent was obtained from the Papal Legate at Durocortorum[56] for the pilgrimage and, to the delight of all the group, for an audience with His Holiness Pope Simplicius. The route to Rome was planned and, in accordance with usual practice, accommodation arranged at abbeys and other religious establishments on the way. All this took weeks of effort to arrange, as communications over long distances were slow and there were many administrative regulations to follow.

In the end, all the arrangements were made and the time came for departure. There was great excitement as Teged set off from Trepunek for his journey to Condate, as the first step of his long journey. Sioned and his family said their farewells with tears all around, but they were also overjoyed for him, as they knew that this was a trip of a lifetime and a spiritual journey of great significance, which few could aspire to. They also knew that long journeys across Gaul and Italia were hazardous, since the time when Rome had lost control of the Empire.

He joined the other pilgrims at Condate in September of the Year of our Lord 482. They travelled in three fine carriages with a team of six guards, plus the coachmen. They were told that trouble was not expected on route, but it was as well to be prepared. Although the route was no longer under Roman control, the first part of the journey was through land controlled by the Franks under the rule of their young king, Clovis. Although not yet a Christian, but a ruthless warrior and ruler, he had much respect for the Church and the role which its bishops played in the administration of the former Roman Empire and in the world as it was at his time. The Franks also did their best to maintain law and order, and to confront and arrest or kill highwaymen and other criminals.

The first main stop for the pilgrims was the Roman City of Caesarodonum[57], at that time under Frankish control. This fine city was situated on either side of the great River Liger[58], which was the longest river in the whole of Gaul apart

---

[56] Rheims

[57] Tours

[58] The Loire

from the Rhenus in the far east of the country. Teged, who loved the River Hafren in his home country, had never seen a river so large and majestic as the Liger at Caesarodonum. There had been a period of heavy rainfall higher up the catchment area of the river, and the river level was higher than usual at that time of the year. Teged was in awe of the power of the flow of water and the relentless roaring sound it made as it raced through the ancient city.

They stayed for two days at the famous monastery of St Martin situated just outside the city. They received a warm welcome there from the monks, and were told something of the life of St Martin. Born in Pannonia[59] to pagan parents, he had converted to Christianity at an early age. He had refused to undertake military service in defiance of the Roman Emperor Julian 'the Apostate' on the grounds that he was a Christian Soldier and was not allowed to fight. This led to conflict and difficulties for him, which in time were resolved. Eventually he became Bishop of Caesarodonum in the year 371 and founded the monastery near the city, where Teged and his fellow pilgrims were now staying on their journey.

They were told that at one stage in his life St Martin had cut his cloak in half in order to give half of it to a beggar. The night after this act, he dreamt that Jesus had restored his cloak to its original condition. When he awoke the next morning, he found that his cloak had indeed been restored. The pilgrims were inspired by this story and also by the spiritual and tranquil quality of the monastery. When they had made a donation to the monastery and said their fond farewells, they set off on the next stage of their journey.

They then had to travel through the part of Gaul allocated to the Visigoths, who were by that time Christians and had due respect for those making a pilgrimage. The journey was slow, since the Roman roads were in a worst state of repair than in earlier times. When the priority is warfare and conflict, sometimes roads can be left to deteriorate. After several days of uneventful travel, that was less than comfortable in carriages on bumpy roads, they travelled through to the land held by the Burgundians and then arrived at Lugdunum[60]. This was still a very large city, having been the capital of a large part of Gaul in Roman times and also one of the main centres of Christianity in the times of terrible persecution before the Emperor Constantine's conversion to that

---

[59] His place of birth is now in Hungary

[60] Lyon

religion. It was now the capital of the Kingdom of the Burgundians and therefore still a very important city.

This was the largest city that Teged had ever seen, and again there was a fine river, which seemed even wider than the Liger. This was the Rhodanus[61], a truly wide river and with many long cargo boats carrying goods down its valley towards the sea. Teged was amazed by everything about this historic city. As they walked about the city, he saw that there was yet another large river[62] there which joined with the other one in the city. He was told that this was just a tributary. He thought it must be by far the largest tributary in the world. Indeed it was much larger than the River Hafren.

At the monastery in the city, he was told something of the history of the region in the early days of Christianity. This included the persecution and execution of Christians there during the reign of the Emperor Marcus Aurelius. There were many martyrs associated with this city.

They were also told of the life and works of the early Christian Bishop Irenaeus of Lugdunum, who was a Greek and had studied under one of the Apostolic Fathers[63], Polycarp. Irenaeus was famous in Christian history for writing an authoritative tract condemning the heresy of Gnosticism entitled 'Against Heresies'. He was a major figure in the establishment of Christianity in Gaul, and in the creation of the Christian canon. Teged had known little or nothing of these matters, but felt inspired to learn of them. He appreciated that even the journey to Rome was in itself educational, given the historic cities along their route to the Holy City, and the knowledge of history and theology retained in the monasteries. Fascinating as this city was for Teged and his fellow pilgrims, it was time to move on. The convoy headed due east with Mediolanum[64] as their next main stop, but on the way there was mountainous terrain to cross, the mighty Alps.

If Teged had been amazed by what he had seen so far on his journey, his first sight of the Alps truly astonished him. He had seen mountains in Britannia, especially in the north of Cambria. It seemed to him that the Alpine peaks reached to the sky. Several were snow-clad, although it was still early autumn. He thought of God delivering the tablets to Moses on a mountain, and how fitting

---

[61] The Rhône

[62] The Saône

[63] These were early Christians who had known one or more of the Apostles

[64] Milan

that was, as there was something monumental and holy about mountains. Teged thought that they were mid-way between Heaven and Earth.

One of the guards who knew the area very well, having grown up in Helvetia[65], told the pilgrims that they would travel through a famous mountain pass called, 'Poeninus Mons'[66]. He explained that, when Julius Caesar first invaded Gaul, this is the route which he took.

Joseph asked, "Did Hannibal also travel on this route when he invaded Italia, bringing elephants with him?"

The guard replied, "He probably did, but I do not know for sure."

Another pilgrim in the party who had studied Roman history interjected, "Yes, that was the route he took and it was also the normal route between Gaul and Italia. If he got his elephants through this pass, we should find it easier in our robust carriages with no responsibilities for other animals."

Teged and his colleagues became more and more excited as they made their way slowly through the pass. The mountains became ever more dominating and impressive. He hoped that the carriages would not break down in this difficult terrain, as it would have been a bleak place to remain stranded hoping for help. Fortunately they travelled safely and eventually arrived at Augusta Praetoria[67]. The journey had been hard and the party took advantage of a long rest at this scenic location.

Their next main stop was Mediolanum, another large and important city, located in a vast and fertile plain. Teged was told by their hosts that this is where Ambrose had been bishop in the days of the Emperor Theodosius. This bishop, he was told, was a very strong and forceful character, and, famously, had required the Emperor to do penance after he had carried out a massacre of civilians at the Greek city of Thessalonica. Ambrose was one of the main influences on the theologian St Augustine of Hippo, and was greatly honoured in Mediolanum. Bishop Joseph told the group of pilgrims that it was at this city that the Emperor Constantine the Great issued the Edict of Toleration, whereby Christianity was permitted to be practised in the Roman Empire. They all came to realise just how important this city had been in the establishment of the Faith in the time of the Roman Empire. This was not just a journey but a voyage through the history of western Christianity.

---

[65] Switzerland

[66] The St Bernard Pass

[67] Aosta

The next stop was Ravenna which had been the last capital of the Western Roman Empire, now no longer in existence after the removal of the last Emperor Romulus Augustus in the year 476. Italia was now under the control of Odoacer, a soldier of Germanic origin, who won power being in command of an army of Romans and Germanic federates of Rome, and who had deposed the last Western Roman Emperor. Odoacer had the support of the Eastern Roman (Byzantine) Emperor at that time. He was by this stage an Arian Christian, and had respect for pilgrims and for the Catholic Church. Consequently, the journey of Teged and his colleagues through Italia was safe and free from any sort of conflict. They were much relieved to have made this long journey without suffering any sort of attack. Although the Pax Romana was no more, the powers now in control of the former Western Roman Empire seemed to have achieved some degree of law and order, such that travel over long distances could still take place in the expectation of a safe passage, particularly for pilgrims on their way to Rome.

Chapter 28
All Roads Lead to Rome

Pilgrimages to Rome were not a new phenomenon and had become more frequent since the time of the Emperor Constantine the Great. Pilgrims came from many parts of Christendom to walk the streets where St Peter and St Paul had trod and to see the many Christian churches and shrines. Some pilgrims also made the long journey to Jerusalem to visit the holy places where Jesus had spent his time in the crucial periods of his life. That journey was much longer and more difficult. There was, however, the Christian belief that the Holy Spirit was everywhere, so that there was no need to go as far as Jerusalem to find it. For many Christians, Rome was nearer to their homes and they were able to make the journey there without too much difficulty. There were reports of some pilgrims behaving badly, both on their way to Rome and when in the Holy City. There was said to be drunkenness, debauchery and worse on the part of some pilgrims, but most behaved respectfully and in ways which might be expected of those coming to worship at holy places.

Because of the large numbers of pilgrims at Rome, arrangements had evolved to cater for their needs, including the provision of accommodation and meals and also for guides to lead them to the various Christian sites. Teged, Joseph and the other pilgrims were all boarded together and cared for in a monastic building in the city, which was by far the largest residential building Teged had ever seen.

And so after their long and tiring journey, Joseph, Teged and their colleagues were safely settled in Rome. In no way did it disappoint: another large city but so very different from the others which Teged had visited. He was spellbound by the sheer size and beauty of this great city. He could hardly make himself believe that he was actually there, in this famous metropolis. There were so many things to see and visit, the Christian sites, in addition to the buildings and ruins from the time of the Roman Republic, and the Empire. He felt that the city was immersed in history. Teged said to Joseph, "I can't help thinking of all the famous people who have walked on these very roads and paths; Julius Caesar, the Emperor Augustus, Cicero, Marcus Antonius, not forgetting the most important of all, St Peter and St Paul and the host of Christian martyrs."

Joseph was equally moved and responded, "The same thoughts came to me, but, as we see, Rome is also a modern bustling and vibrant city. Despite being sacked on various occasions, with buildings destroyed, wealth stolen and citizens taken as slaves, much still remains for us to appreciate and admire. The influence of the Holy Catholic Church is, of course, everywhere, like a bright beacon illuminating Christendom." Teged and the others nodded showing their approval to this latter comment.

The group of pilgrims were provided with guides, the chief of whom was called Eusebius. He was originally from Greece but had lived in Rome for several years and knew the city and all its important sites very well. He spoke good Latin but with a hint of a Greek accent. Eusebius commented on the conduct of certain pilgrims and was pleased to see that Bishop Joseph's group were devout people who had come to Rome to show due respect to the holy sites. When he first met them, Eusebius addressed them, "One of the problems with so many pilgrims coming here is the removal of relics, anything which people believed had some connection with Christ, the saints or the martyrs. They might be splinters of wood, pieces of fabric or ampules of oil from tombs. There is also a trade in selling bogus relics to gullible pilgrims. Some years ago, Bishop Achilleus and other Church leaders have warned against pagan-like superstition in cults of relics."

Bishop Joseph replied, "I am sure that none of us are minded to take anything from holy sites other than divine inspiration that such places will grant to us."

Of the ecclesiastical buildings which they visited, they were much inspired by the Basilica of St Peter, built in the previous century by the Emperor Constantine. The building was truly magnificent: as its name suggested it was palatial and regal but at the same time spiritual and ecclesiastical. It was not just the building itself but its associations. It was built near the place where St Peter had been crucified at the time of the Emperor Nero, who had blamed the Christians for the terrible fire which had ravaged the city. So many were martyred at that terrible time. What was foremost in the thoughts of Teged was that the Basilica was dedicated to the disciple who was the first Bishop of Rome and succeeded by Popes, including the one who would shortly grant them an audience. It was almost too much for Teged, a farmer and horse-breeder from Britannia now settled in Armorica, to take in. He felt that he was at the very centre of the world, whilst his birthplace and his current home were on the periphery of civilisation.

Another highlight was the guided tour of the Catacombs, where many Christian martyrs had been laid to rest. The guides drew their attention to the many inscriptions on the walls of the Catacombs regarding those laid to rest there. Eusebius told them that there were no less than three hundred martyrs killed at Rome whose feasts were celebrated annually by the Church.

The group of pilgrims were escorted along the Via Ostiensis to the shrine to St Paul and along the Via Appia to that of St Sebastian.

Of the many pagan sites, Teged was very impressed with the Colosseum, not only the beauty of the architecture but the insight it gave to life in Rome during the imperial period, as a venue for entertainment of many kinds, some of which involved the ghastly slaughter of Christians.

The Pantheon also stood out for him: once dedicated to the pagan gods, it was now a Christian site. They saw as many ancient sites as time would allow, including the various Forums and the Circus Maximus. He and Joseph came to realise how devoted the Romans had been to their own pre-Christian pantheistic religion. This was obvious to see from all the ruined shrines to Roman gods and goddesses. Joseph explained to Teged that, like many ancient peoples, the Romans were very superstitious; hence their wish always to please their gods and to consult soothsayers and prophets. They believed that disrespect to one of their deities could lead to disaster.

One thing that surprised Teged was the variety of different peoples in the city. At its busy markets, one could hear many people speaking Greek and many others using the languages and dialects of the various Germanic communities. As well as Christian churches, there were synagogues attended by Jews still settled in the city and running businesses there. Joseph pointed out that some of these Jewish people were speaking Hebrew or Aramaic, languages spoken by Christ himself.

There were many people with dark skins, which Teged assumed were from Africa or Asia. Some spoke languages which he had never heard before and the origins of which he could not even guess at. He spoke to Joseph about this and his learned response was, "We must remember the Jesus himself, St Peter and St Paul were all from what we now call Palestine and were not of the European race. Their skins may have been darker than ours. They would also have conversed in Aramaic or Hebrew, (like the Jews here now) and would surely also have been familiar with Latin and Greek. Some of the languages now spoken here are from African lands where Christianity spread in the days of the early church. It was in Egypt, for example, that St Timothy founded monasticism in Christendom."

Teged as always was impressed with his friend's knowledge of such matters.

Teged was also amazed by the clothes that some of the people were wearing, some in very fine fabrics. He noticed wealthy ladies wearing garments of exquisite silks, something rarely if ever seen at home. He commented on this to Joseph, as they strolled along taking in the sights.

Joseph explained that for centuries Rome had imported silk, jade and other luxury items from the east of Asia, along land routes known as the *Silk Roads*. He added, "Some say that the taste for such luxury goods was a factor in the decline and fall of the Western Roman Empire. We must all take care therefore to value virtue and charity ahead of all such vanity and luxuries."

Whilst taking due heed of this sound advice, at a busy market, Teged purchased a few luxury items as presents for Sioned, when he got back home. He missed her very much and wanted to take her something really special and which might make her appreciate how different Rome was to their home town in Armorica.

The thing which shocked Teged most at Rome was the widespread incidence of prostitution. In the evening it was visible everywhere, in all busy areas where customers may be looking for that service. They were even to be seen on the Via Aurelia, the route leading to St Peter's Basilica. He had seen prostitutes on the streets in Britannia, especially in garrison towns, but not so blatant and prominent. Many of the prostitutes were smartly dressed but in a way which made it obvious why there were there. Some seemed very young. There were also mature women, who looked no longer at their most enticing for this oldest of professions. He was utterly shocked to see young men and boys, who were also said to be male prostitutes.

Teged and Joseph were in no way tempted by what was being offered. It was a fact, however, that some pilgrims were led into temptation in this Holy City. Teged said to his colleague and to Eusebius, "It is disgraceful that such conduct is allowed in this Holy City. These people should be locked up in prison."

Eusebius responded, "Many would agree with you, but bear in mind most are not out there from choice. Some will be under the control of evil pimps or slave masters, keen to make money from their demeaning activities. Others may be living in abject poverty, with this activity as the only way of providing food and shelter for themselves and perhaps their children. Poverty and prostitution have always gone together, but happily most poor people seem to get by in other ways."

Joseph concurred with these comments.

Teged response was, "Yes, gentlemen, I am sure you are right. I should be more understanding and forgiving. But it is so wrong that it should be going on at Rome of all places. I hope that the Catholic Church is doing all it can to help the poor and needy and to drive prostitution from the streets."

Eusebius answered, "I fear that some in our Church have their eyes set on wealth and privilege, which diverts them from the paths of righteousness."

Joseph added, "I am told, however, on good authority that His Holiness is a man of simplicity, who spends his time in study and prayer, avoiding all the trappings of wealth and luxury. This is also clear from his own writings and from what others have said about him. He did not come from a monastic background, but from what I have heard he lives in a monastic way. This does not, however, mean that all in authority lead such devoted lives."

These comments made Teged think deeply about the forthcoming meeting with the Pope. He was very excited and a little apprehensive when the day of his audience with the Pope arrived. He need not have worried as the Holy Father, who was amicable and understanding, immediately put Teged at his ease. What Joseph had said about him seemed absolutely true. The audience was a tranquil and reflective meeting between two men in the later stages of their lives. Before receiving the Papal blessing, His Holiness asked Teged about his family and about life in Britannia and in Armorica. Teged informed him that he was married to Sioned and that they had three children and several grandchildren. He added that they all attended the little church in their town every Sunday for the Eucharist. He said that their presbyter was a very learned man, celibate and a devout Christian.

He told His Holiness that he missed his place of birth, Britannia, but that Armorica was a more peaceful place, under less threat from invaders. The Pope mentioned the missions of Bishop Germanus to Britannia and expressed his relief that its people had been saved from the heresy of Pelagianism. He also expressed the hope that one day the Saxons would be converted to the Faith. He said that he believed that the Faith was like a powerful tide which would in time carry the whole world with it by virtue of its irresistible message. Teged politely agreed with these sentiments, which he hoped would prove correct.

When he joined the others, Teged felt uplifted in the knowledge that he had spoken with a successor of St Peter. He regarded the Pope as a man of simplicity and at the same time of great depth in the Faith and his understanding of the world.

Chapter 29
The Port of Rome

Teged was sad at heart to leave Rome, as he knew he would never see it again. But to see it once was a huge boon for him, and the city had made a massive impression on him. He could still see its buildings, ancient and more modern in his mind's eye and believed that these would for ever be etched in his memory. Even more so would be the voice and pious dignity of the Pontiff.

As with many large cities there was good and bad there, and extremes of wealth and poverty. His main feeling was that it was indeed the Holy City. Joseph whole-heartedly agreed with that sentiment and also saw Rome as a fertile place for Christianity to take root, as it had been the centre for the pre-Christian religions and sects. It had always been a place where people had been searching for meaning and answers to the most difficult questions facing the human race. The true Faith now showed them the way and had spread to the world through the reach of the Roman Empire.

Teged, who loved rivers, was a little disappointed with the Tiber, which was not beautiful like the Hafren nor majestic like the great rivers he had seen in Gaul. The weather had been warm and dry and the water level in the Tiber was lower than usual, which partly explained its lack of attraction to Teged: in a few places it seemed to him not much more than a trickle of tepid water over warm smooth stones.

At a rather more prosaic level, he also felt that the fish markets at Rome did not compare with those in Armorica. At the main Roman market, the fish were small and mainly confined to red mullet and bream. In Armorica, the fish markets offered large bass, turbot, brill, sole, halibut, as well as scallops, eels, oysters and mussels. However, much of the fruit and vegetables at the markets were superb, of fine quality and with a much greater variety than those in Armorica. The guide told Teged that the fish market at Ostia had large tuna and swordfish most weeks.

Whilst thinking of these markets, he also reflected on the excellent fare that they had dined on during the long journey and at Rome itself. As well as good meat, fish and bread, there had been plenty of fresh fruit and vegetables, as they travelled further south into warmer climes. There was nothing quite like the plump grapes freshly picked in vineyards belonging to the monasteries where they stayed. He also tasted peaches for the first time in his life and much enjoyed this delicious and refreshing fruit. There was home-made beer at some monasteries as well as cider and, of course, fine local wine, especially in the southern lands of Gaul and northern Italia.

Despite his great appreciation of Rome and all the other great cities which he had visited, he was keen to get back home to his family in Trepunek. It came as a complete surprise when Joseph told him that they were returning home by sea, which should be quicker. He did not know what to say in response, but his mind turned to the excellent guards, who had served them well, and to the carriages.

"What will happen to the fine carriages and those excellent guards?" he asked.

Joseph, who always kept himself well informed as a good bishop should be, replied, "I am told that they will be taking a group of the clergy and missionaries to northern Gaul as part of a major campaign to convert the leaders of the Franks to Christianity. There are already many Christians in northern Gaul, including some Frankish people, but their leaders are yet to be converted. I pray that things might change for the better soon. Powerful and devout rulers of men in partnership with the Catholic Church will be beneficial for all mankind in temporal and spiritual matters.

"As for our group of mankind, tomorrow we are going to travel in other coaches to the Port of Rome[68], where we shall embark on a large merchant ship to take us back to Armorica. Our first port of call will be Massilia[69] where I am told we will take on more provisions."

"Is the Port of Rome the place at the mouth of the River Tiber known as Ostia? I think that this is what I was taught when studying Latin at Deva and also what Eusebius told us."

"It was in the past and there is still a busy port there and a fishing harbour, but the Emperor Trajan built a much larger and deeper harbour for the biggest

---

[68] Civitavecchia

[69] Marseille

vessels at a site about forty miles north of Rome, which is now the main port of the city."

The day came and the pilgrims arrived at the fine new Port of Rome, with mixed emotions about a long sea voyage. Some feared storms and sea-sickness. Some felt that even on a large vessel they might feel cramped. No one, however, complained, as the journey over land had been long and arduous. In some ways a sea voyage might even be a bit more comfortable. At least they hoped so. A few including Teged were really excited at the prospect of boarding a large vessel and seeing foreign lands from the open sea. He had never heard of Massilia and asked Joseph about it. He was always well informed and responded, "It is a busy port in the south of Provincia[70], which was colonised by the Greeks many centuries ago. It is in a crucial location on routes by sea to North Africa and to Italia and Hispania. It was captured and held by the Romans for centuries but is now under Visigoth control as part of the land allocated to them at the last days of the Roman Empire."

There were several large ships moored at the Port of Rome, as well as a host of other vessels, both medium sized and small. All sorts of goods were being unloaded from some of the ships. Joseph said that one of the large ships was being unloaded with wheat and other cereals from Egypt, destined for Rome and other large Italian cities.

Filled with excitement and anxiety, they were directed to their ship and embarked. It looked truly magnificent with its fine timber and lofty masts. It would look even better when at sea and in full sail.

They were welcomed aboard by its captain, a stocky and rugged-looking Italian called Marius, who had sailed both warships and cargo vessels for the last twenty years through very turbulent times. In his career, he had sailed as far as Cornubia to deliver products from the Mediterranean and to bring back copper, tin, iron and lead to Hispania and to Italian ports. He had also sailed east as far as Tyre and Sidon, the home of the Phoenicians and two of the main gateways to the east. He had regularly sailed back from Alexandria in Egypt with a cargo of grain for the Roman market. Marius was a man of massive upper body strength, gained from hauling ropes and pulling up heavy anchors. His legs were also powerful, resembling tree trunks.

---

[70] This means 'the Province' in Latin, which gave its name to Provence.

On this current voyage there were other passengers aboard, apart from the homeward-bound pilgrims, and also a cargo of fine pottery, marble and luxury goods to deliver to Massilia. As they put to sea, for most passengers the worst fears of sea-sickness were dispelled as the sea was calm and the voyage was pleasant, with fine views of the distant countryside, but with light winds progress was slow. During these long hours, Teged and Joseph had many lengthy conversations about the state of the world and regarding religion. They discussed what the Pope had said about converting other peoples to the Faith. They both hoped that the Saxons and the Franks would in time become Christian. Perhaps the latest mission to northern Gaul would achieve success.

Since visiting Rome, it seemed that everything which Teged saw reminded him of stories from the Bible, which he had known from his early life in Britannia. Now they were at sea, with an abundance of enthusiasm but with a total absence of tact, he said to Joseph, "This journey we are on now calls to mind the voyage of St Paul from Palestine to Rome and of the terrible shipwreck which occurred, perhaps in Cyprus."

Joseph responded, with more than a hint of anxiety in his voice, "That is a pious thought, Teged, but not a very cheerful one, particularly for people like me who have never been on a long sea voyage before. But at least St Paul survived and reached Rome. Let us hope that we will get to Armorica without too much trouble."

"I am sorry, but since being in Rome I am always thinking of events recorded in the Bible. Remember that our Lord walked on the water in the Sea of Galilee."

"I am a man of strong faith but even mine is not strong enough to try walking on these waters. I cannot even swim."

"I wasn't suggesting that we should try to walk on the water. I was just thinking of our Lord. I am fortunate to be able to swim, as my dear father taught all his children to swim. With fast flowing and deep rivers and also lakes in our homeland, our father thought it necessary for us to be able to swim. It was also a very pleasant pastime for us. I do not know how I would fare if I tried to swim in the sea this far from land. It was not something I would try."

As the journey progressed, the majestic vessel passed between two large land masses, and Teged asked a young member of the crew what these were. The young man, whose name was Gracchus, was a nephew of the captain and had sailed on several voyages with him. He replied, "Sir, they are two large islands, called Corsica to the right and Sardinia to the left. When we have passed through these straits, we shall travel north-west towards Massilia. The wind usually freshens once we have passed this area and we might then make better progress."

"Thank you. What will we find at Massilia?"

"I have been there several times. It is a large and busy city with people from various countries there. The port is a main feature of the city for passenger and cargo ships, and for fishing boats. My cousins are fishermen there and bring fish to the market most days. We will know that we are on the right course when we see the huge rocky outcrop in the city, which can be seen from miles away and has always been a vital landmark for sailors. From Massilia one can travel by sea to all the main places on the Mediterranean. Before we get quite that far west there can be good views of the lofty Alps on a clear day. I always love those views."

"Thank you again. We will look forward to our visit there. I hope we can get to the fish market and see what the catch has brought in."

The weather remained warm and calm and progress was too slow until galley slaves were put to work to propel the vessel along with their long oars. Teged was uneasy about the use of slaves and spoke about it to Joseph, who was of the same view. Joseph said, "I cannot reconcile slavery with the Gospels, but it will be many years before men will banish it. In the meantime, we should treat slaves as fairly as we can and give them their freedom when we have the chance to do so."

Teged agreed and thought of his slaves, whom he had freed. He felt too modest to mention it, but Joseph was aware of what his friend had done and greatly respected him for it.

As the voyage proceeded, Teged and his colleagues were thrilled to see the Alps again from so far away. In some ways this view was even more moving than seeing them from close at hand. They looked surreal and magical to these travellers, rising above some of the cloud cover, and snow-capped.

They arrived safely at Massilia, which was indeed a large and bustling city, with people from many lands. The pilgrims visited some of its places of interest, including its cathedral, where they received a warm welcome from the bishop, who told them he was from Athens.

The bishop had heard of Armorica but not of Britannia, which he imagined to be in southern Italia. Teged explained to him its location and told him about the Saxon invasion and why so many people had migrated to Gaul. The bishop was annoyed to learn that people of the Faith should be displaced in this way. A deacon from Burgundy, who was better informed, explained the recent history in great detail to the bishop, who was grateful and shocked at the same time. The well-informed deacon also mentioned the missions of Bishop Germanus to combat Pelagianism. The Athenian bishop had no idea that Christianity had existed in such northern lands. He was then told of Bishop Patrick's mission to Hibernia. The bishop from Athens had heard of this place, but, like the Romans, he thought it was full of monsters. He was so pleased to know that there were now monasteries there dedicated to prayer and the study of sacred texts. The Athenian bishop, with the famous humour of Attica, liked a pun and joked, "The monsters have been superseded by monasteries." Polite laughter ensued.

The time came for them to begin the next stage of the sea voyage to Gades[71], a port city in the far south of Hispania facing the Great Ocean. The captain mentioned to Joseph, whom he regarded as the leader of the pilgrims, that they were now carrying a precious cargo of gold and silver coins for delivery to the Visigoth Ruler of the region of Gades. He added that this information should be kept confidential. There was a risk of piracy. There were a number of extra armed guards aboard in case of trouble. The captain did not want to let the passengers know in case it might cause anxiety. He added, "I have dealt with pirates many times in the past and know how to combat them effectively. I also have some well-trained guards on board. I am not expecting trouble, but it as well to be prepared for all that fortune might throw at us."

Joseph, who was to some extent reassured, mentioned this in strict confidence to Teged, who thought that this is just one more hazard on the open sea, and he hoped that they would not have to face it. Fortunately he could not remember any reference to pirates in the New Testament: otherwise he might have had another troubling story to tell. Teged had thought of Jonah and the whale but did not raise that subject as up to that time they had not seen any of these large creatures on the voyage. Later on they did indeed see some massive and majestic sea creatures. When they appeared, Gracchus told them, "These are Orcas, otherwise known as killer whales. Don't go for a swim when they are in the vicinity. They have also been known to try to overturn small boats, and terrify the occupants. We are much too big for them to try to capsize us!"

Joseph, Teged and the others were amazed by this information. They were also greatly impressed by the beauty of these large animals.

---

[71] Cadiz

Neither he nor Joseph carried any weapons, as this would have been incompatible with a pilgrimage. The sea was not, however, under the strict control of the Romans, the Visigoths, the Vandals, the Byzantines or anyone else, but a place where pirates could chance their luck. The two wished they had their swords with them, just in case of trouble.

Chapter 30
Trouble at Sea

The vessel set sail from Massilia aided by a brisk easterly wind and with no need for oarsmen. It was a magnificent sight in full sail. There was a cargo of pottery, wine and spices, and also the valuable coins which were hidden away in an iron safe. There were around fifty passengers on board including the pilgrims. Many of the pilgrims were by now getting more accustomed to and comfortable with the prospect of a long sea voyage. They were all impressed with the rugged captain and his crew.

All was quiet and peaceful, until the ship was near to the Fretum Gaditanum,[72] when suddenly the left-side lookout reported two ships approaching at speed from the direction of Mauritania. The captain half expected piracy, but wondered whether these potential pirates had information about the cargo or whether they were just chancers. As he had told Joseph, he was prepared for all eventualities, having commanded warships as well as merchant vessels.

He immediately called an alert and ordered all passengers to go below forthwith. Armed guards were placed outside the storeroom where the coins were kept. There were also twenty armed guards on the deck, with shields and swords. Gracchus was also present there to give his support to his uncle. The slaves were kept locked away. It was unpredictable what might happen if they got involved in conflict. They might side with the pirates if they thought it would be a route to freedom. On the other hand, even if they survived, there was no guarantee that ruthless pirates would treat them any better than their current owners.

As the two ships drew nearer, it became very clear that they were hostile. When in range, their crew started to fire arrows, with great accuracy. Some guards were hit and fell. Then the ships drew close enough for boarding to begin

---

[72] The Straits of Gibraltar

and pirates swarmed on to the ship. An intense battle with swords and spears flared up with casualties on both sides. The passengers below were terrified, hearing the clash of arms and cries and screams from the wounded. The captain fought like a lion and killed several pirates, but feared that the battle was not going his way.

Joseph and Teged could not contain themselves and felt impelled to go on deck and help as much as they could. They pushed past the guards and got onto the deck.

Although no longer young men, they were both fit and well, and knew how to handle swords, through their respective experiences in warfare. They were joined by another pilgrim from Condate, a younger man called Gaius, who also wanted to help but who had never been in any militia. Joseph and Teged both grabbed swords which had fallen from wounded guards and went to battle with the pirates. Both men were skilled warriors and it soon showed as they killed several pirates or caused them to jump overboard to their fate in the cold open sea.

Gaius tried to emulate Joseph and Teged, by taking a sword and facing the pirates, but his inexperience showed. He was too slow and did not see a pirate closing in on him. Teged tried to help, but Gaius was slain by a pirate spear, which penetrated his back and entered his heart. Teged was filled with intense anger, which showed in his eyes; he sought out and slew the killer, a young man hardly old enough to grow a beard. There was another tragedy; young Gracchus suffered a wound in his thigh and lost much blood. Despite the efforts of a surgeon to stem the flow of blood, the young man died immediately after the battle. Marius was mortified with grief and wept bitter tears. He had feelings of guilt at allowing the young man to remain on deck. He felt that he should have left defence of the vessel to the older armed guards. He had also not foreseen how fierce the battle with the pirates would be.

Some of the other pirates seemed very young and had the appearance of North Africans. Their leader, who rushed back to his ship, as soon as he saw that he was losing the battle, seemed to be speaking in the tongue of the Vandals, who now had a kingdom in North Africa.

The terrible episode was intense but time had flown by and it seemed that the battle was over almost as quickly as it had begun. Joseph and Teged took no pride in killing pirates, but felt that they had done their duty. The captain still in deep grief could not praise them enough, "Your intervention, gentlemen, made the difference, and swung the battle in our favour. You handled swords and shields with great skill. I am fortunate that you were aboard. You must have fought wars in your younger days."

Joseph said in a sombre voice, "That is correct. But before I say anymore, I bitterly regret the loss of your fine young nephew. I will pray to the Lord for his soul and that he may have eternal life.

"As for me, when I was young and before I took holy orders, I fought under the Roman Consul Flavius Aëtius at the great battle against Attila the Hun. My friend Teged fought in many conflicts with the Saxons in Britannia. We do not engage in warfare or in violence of any kind, except in self-defence and in the most exceptional circumstances. We have travelled all the way from Armorica to Rome over land with no threat from anyone, but the open sea is a different matter, which is hard to police. We shall pray for God's forgiveness and for the souls of all those who have sadly died on this terrible day. We bitterly regret the loss of the pilgrim Gaius and weep for him and his family. We will pray that law and order will prevail on the high seas, as in olden times when Pompeius the Great drove all pirates from the Mediterranean."

The wounded received treatment as far as possible on the ship and the deceased were all buried at sea, whether pirates or crew members. Bishop Joseph said the last rites for them all, with great sincerity and dignity.

All the passengers from below had come back on deck. Some were physically sick at the sight of the dead and wounded, and on seeing so much blood on the deck. The crew set to the job of clearing blood and gore from the deck with seawater. It seemed that it might have been something they had done several times before.

The voyage continued with a great sense of loss and sadness all around and in fear of some further attack. Soon they reached the Fretum Gaditanum and saw the magnificent sight of the Columnae Herculis.[73] Their excitement at the sight of these famous locations was severely tempered by the terrible events earlier that day. It was surely a day which none of them would ever forget, but might never wish to talk about.

---

[73] The Pillars of Hercules

Chapter 31
Homeward-Bound

With a strong following wind, they eventually arrived at the port of Gadez. Teged had never heard of this city, although it was probably the oldest inhabited city in the whole of Europe. The captain, who had been there many times, knew something of its history and was pleased to tell Joseph and Teged about it. Marius was still deeply in mourning, but it helped him to spend a few moments on other things. He replied, "They say that it was founded by the Phoenicians more than one thousand years before the birth of Christ. These people were the great sailors and traders of the ancient world, who came originally from Tyre and Sidon. They travelled all over the Mediterranean and as far as Britannia, an amazing achievement in those primitive times. The Carthaginians captured Gadez and settled here, in view of its important maritime location. Later, it became Roman and the great Julius Caesar was based here for a while. He granted Roman citizenship to all its freemen.

"Then came the Vandals and later the Visigoths, who are now in control of the city and its region. It once had many ancient temples and statues, but the city suffered serious damage when captured by the Romans and later by the Visigoths."

Joseph and Teged were grateful for this information and felt amazed that they were now in the oldest inhabited city in the continent. It seemed to be surrounded by sea on all sides and was not large in area but densely populated. Again many languages were spoken there: Latin, Gothic, Greek, and those which appeared to be from Africa.

A vibrant place, it was rather exposed to the west wind, which was blowing strongly at the time of their visit. This gave the passengers some cause for alarm as to what the conditions might be like when they ventured onto the Great Ocean, well beyond the Mediterranean.

The captain was relieved to see the valuable coins being taken from the ship by the heavily armed agents of the Visigoth Ruler of the province. The task was carried out in an unobtrusive way, so as not to attract the attention of any potential criminal elements. Most of the passengers did not know what was happening.

Some of the passengers disembarked as the city was their final destination. A few new passengers embarked for the journey to Naoned. Of these, two were scribes and scholars who were expert in classical Greek and Latin texts and were on their way to the monastery at Ponterle to assist Abbot Clement in his studies. It was a great benefit that they were able to read and write in Greek, both of the classical period and of the time of the New Testament. That prestigious and ancient tongue had evolved and changed over the five hundred years from the time of Pericles to the age of St Paul.

The captain took on a large quantity of food and drink for the last long stage of the journey to Armorica, as there were many mouths to feed and many days ahead. He was not yet decided on the route. He could either take the most direct route on the Great Ocean, in the hope that there would be no severe gales, or otherwise the safer option of hugging the coasts of Hispania and Gaul. If he kept near to the coast, he would, however, have to cope with very strong tides in some locations, particularly where there were headlands. He had made this journey many times and his instinct as to the best route usually proved correct.

They had to remain in the city for a few days longer than intended, as it was experiencing the first severe gale of the autumn. This battered the city, its buildings and its trees. Teged thought, *it is just as bad if not worse than the gales we experience in Armorica.*

When at last they set sail, Captain Marius decided to keep within sight of the shore for the first part of the voyage, in case they might need to get quickly into a harbour or safe anchorage. They made steady progress heading north along the west coast of Lusitania[74] and Hispania and then entered the Mare Cantabricum,[75] where unusually the weather conditions were very clement, with fine days and a good and stiff south-westerly wind. Most nights, there were clear skies with hundreds of stars to observe. This made navigation very easy; the Pole Star was usually clearly visible on such nights. The captain had taken the decision to stay well out at sea, so as to take the shortest route. This turned out

---

[74] Latin name for Portugal

[75] The Roman name for the Bay of Biscay.

to be a good choice. There was only one day of strong winds, which the stout vessel easily coped with. The passengers were again impressed both with the ship and with the skill and dedication of the crew.

Eventually the ship reached its destination, the small port of Corbilo[76], situated at the mouth of the River Liger and the nearest port to Naoned.

The passengers disembarked in fine weather on a late autumn morning. They thanked the captain and crew in effusive and very sincere terms. Those who had never been to sea before were more than grateful to have arrived safely on dry land and in the region which most of them called home. The weary passengers made their way over land to their respective destinations in Armorica. There were warm embraces between the captain and Teged and Joseph: with emotions felt by all three after the pirate attack and the loss of Gaius and of Gracchus.

Then Teged and Joseph bid a fond farewell to each other and pledged to meet up soon with friends and family to tell them all about the wonderful pilgrimage. Bishop Joseph with several other pilgrims headed for Condate. Gradually Teged got his land legs back and went on his homeward journey to Trepunek.

---

[76] There was said to be a Gaulish Armorican port of this name where St Nazaire is now situated.

Chapter 32
News Awaits in Armorica

It was cold and wet when Teged's hired carriage arrived at his estate in Trepunek. How modest and simple the whole area looked to him after the sights and sounds of the vast continent and the open sea through which he had travelled. But nothing in those great lands compared with the fact that this was his home, where he would find his beloved wife and children, not forgetting dear Uncle Maldwyn, the man of a thousand stories. Teged now felt himself a match for his uncle as a raconteur with his own accounts of about the various stages of the adventure, about which he looked forward to telling Uncle Maldwyn, hoping to amaze him.

When Sioned came out to meet him, she rushed into his arms with tears of joy overwhelming her eyes. They sat together and drank some wine. He saw that the delight in her face at seeing him was tempered by a hint of sadness. Speaking sorrowfully, she told the sad news, "I am sorry to tell you that Uncle Maldwyn has passed away. He had not been too well for a few weeks. He still enjoyed talking to his family and friends as always; stories about his youth in Britannia and about battles with the Saxons and other invaders. One evening after along and cheerful discussion, he decided to take to his bed early, and died peacefully in his sleep. He was laid to rest in the cemetery, with the last rites spoken by the Presbyter Daniel."

Teged was lost for words. Maldwyn had been part of his life for ever. They grew even closer after Teged's father, Geraint, had died. Maldwyn had been fit and well earlier in the season when they had departed for Rome. Feeling overcome with shock and grief, he whispered to Sioned, "I am distraught that I was not here to say farewell to him. Was I selfish to journey to far off lands and to neglect those nearest to me?"

"No, my dear. A pilgrimage to the Holy City is one of the most sacred and duteous things any Christian could ever do. You went away with all our love and very best wishes, including those of our dear uncle. There was no way that any of us wanted to prevent you going. I am so grateful that you have returned to us safe and sound. None of us, in fact, said farewell to Uncle Maldwyn, as he seemed quite well when he went to his bed. I have more news for you, but first I am desperate to know all about your pilgrimage."

They hugged again in a long embrace. They were so relieved and happy to be together again. Sounding a little weary, Teged continued, "It will take a long time and I am now very weary after the long journey. I will tell you more later on, but I would say that I received the blessing of His Holiness the Pope at my audience. He also blessed you, my dear, and all our family. I have seen great cities, including Rome, and majestic rivers. I have travelled through the lofty Alps, which are taller than you could imagine and snow-capped even in autumn. We returned home by sea in a mighty vessel, with a captain, as skilful and brave as a human being can ever be.

"I have some gifts for you which I purchased at a huge market in Rome."

With an affectionate smile, he handed Sioned a beautiful shawl made of real silk of the highest quality, and some fine jewellery.

She was deeply moved and with tears in her eyes said, "This is the most gorgeous garment I have ever seen. It is so wonderful to look at and to touch. I also love the jewellery. I am so grateful."

She kissed him tenderly.

She could not help seeing how fatigued he was. She served him some food and then he took to his bed for a long sleep.

The next morning he rose early feeling greatly refreshed after a deep sleep in his own bed.

When they were having their first meal of the day, he asked his wife how the children were. Before she replied, he saw the sadness in her eyes. She found it hard to tell him what had happened. Struggling for several moments to find the words, she said, "Geraint and Nessa are both well and are here, but Cadwur with his young son Kitto have gone to Britannia to join in the struggle against the Saxons." She could hardly utter the words, as the news was so sad to relate. She had to stop herself and could not say any more.

Teged was surprised to the core and utterly shocked by this news. He took a few moments to take it all in.

"How on Earth did this come to pass?"

Having given the news, Sioned composed herself and tried to explain, "I am not sure I have got all the details right but it seems that the chief ruler in power in Britannia is now a noble of Roman and British descent called Ambrosius Aemilianus.[77] They say that he is the son of Ambrosius, who once sought refuge in Armorica and who later fought against Vortigern and defeated him. The new chief ruler has been rallying support from all the militias in Britannia to make a great effort to push back the Saxons. A mission was sent to Armorica to enlist the support of trained soldiers to go to Britannia to join the great army being created by the chief ruler. They were particularly interested in cavalry officers, who could both fight and train others. Cadwur and his friend dear Matthew were amongst the first to enlist. The young Kitto, who is so very skilled as a rider, repeatedly begged his father to let him join the group and I bitterly regret to say that his father foolishly conceded and consented to him doing so.

"Nessa, Morwenna and I were all distraught, and so of course was Rhian, who was being separated from her husband and young son. I have cried bitter tears every day since their departure. I fear we shall never see them again, whether they win or lose in the battles which are to come. I hope and pray that I am wrong about this."

Teged too was utterly dejected and shared his wife's sentiments. He recalled his brother Owain's letter inviting him to come to Armorica to escape the dangers at home, and yet his own son and grandson had answered a call to arms in that very hazardous land, when they could have lived in peace at Trepunek. He also grieved for his niece, Morwenna, a mother with several children, who now had to live on without her husband and would always fear for his survival. She had also lost both of her parents, Owain and Gwen. Teged was minded to do whatever he could to support her and likewise Rhian and her children.

The news, first the death of Maldwyn and then the departure of Cadwur and Kitto, had taken away the feeling of elation which Teged had from the pilgrimage and the safe return home.

He recalled how his warrior son Cadwur had always wanted to go to the Gododdin to meet the horsemen of the Votadini. He and his father-in-law, Bran, had no doubt shared their enthusiasm for this area with the young and impressionable Kitto. Teged also remembered how his nephew, the older Kitto

---

[77] Ambrosius and his son are in the area of myth rather than history.

The military support from Armorica to Britannia is not supported by any evidence and is therefore fiction.

143

the son of Owain, had died after a battle wound. He hoped that the young man of the same name would not suffer the same fate. *I hope history will not repeat itself,* he thought.

He knew that Cadwur was a trained and highly skilled warrior, who knew how to fight and was mature enough to make his own decisions, but his son was young and impressionable with all his life before him. He was far too young to die or to be put in peril. Teged felt intensely angry with Cadwur for not insisting that the young Kitto remain at home with his family. There was nothing he could do about it now. They were across the wide sea and hundreds of miles away in a distant land.

Life was now sombre for the family of Teged, and that of Matthew. Owain's family were also very upset and anxious.

Over the next few days the family became a little more contented as Teged told them in detail of his journey to Rome and his homeward sea voyage. He had so much of interest to tell them that for a time it took their minds off Cadwur and Kitto. They were impressed with all he had to say, about cities, monasteries, landscape and rivers, and the mountains. They were most interested in hearing his description of the City of Rome and of his audience with the Pope. Sioned was filled with joy on hearing that she and the children had also received the blessing of the Holy Father.

Like Teged, they had not expected a sea voyage as a feature in the itinerary. Teged had obviously enjoyed that part of the journey and his sense of adventure clearly showed in his account of the events. He rather skated over the attack by pirates referring to it as a minor inconvenience. He did not mention his part in it nor all the fatalities and gory scenes. That was just as well, as Sioned was horrified even by his brief account to think that he might have been killed by pirates.

A few weeks later, there was a visit from Bishop Joseph and a group of other pilgrims from Condate. Teged and Sioned laid on a banquet for them, after which each pilgrim gave his account of the pilgrimage to the group of friends and relations.

Life got back more or less to normal for Teged and his family. The estate was well managed by his son Geraint, and Nessa continued to excel as a breeder of horses, many of which she and her husband Medar sold at good prices. But nothing could make up for the absence of those who had gone to Britannia and for the very real fears for their safety, which continued to trouble Teged like black clouds in a threatening sky. Teged's hair had been turning grey for some years but it was now becoming snow white from his constant thoughts of his son and grandson in Britannia.

Chapter 33
Kitto is put to the Test

In that same year 482, the group of soldiers of which Cadwur, Kitto and Matthew were a part, had sailed from Tregaran to a small port on the estuary at the head of which was the city of Isca[78]. Its name in the British language was Caer Uisc, meaning the city on the water: the River Exe.

They disembarked from the ship and made their way over land the short distance to the city of Isca, where they saw that there were Roman walls and a Roman castle, the latter now occupied by a Dumnonian militia. Over the last few decades many Britons had travelled to Isca to get away from the Saxon settlers and invaders. They had planned to settle either in Dumnonia, Cornubia or across the sea in Armorica. Isca was a busy and crowded city. It was a travel hub and a centre for commerce but also for religion. It did not at that time have a cathedral or bishop but there was a church in the city. It was a building which previously had been a pagan temple and was converted into a church in the fourth century. There was also a once-imposing Roman bathhouse at the centre of the city, which sadly had become rather derelict since the time when the Roman legion based there had left the area to go to Gaul.

Cadwur thought it was a fine city and particularly admired what remained of the Roman architecture, as well as the setting of the city nestling in green and wooded hills to the north and west.

The group then travelled over land in carriages and some on horseback to the north of Dumnonia from where they sailed over to Menevia[79]. They then travelled

---

[78] Exeter

[79] This was a diocese in South Wales of which St David became Bishop in the early sixth century.

to the former Roman fortress town of Caerlegeion[80] situated alongside another River Uisc. This was a substantial town with many Roman buildings still standing, including a Roman bathhouse, now a little dilapidated and fine amphitheatre.

A shock awaited Cadwur and Kitto. They were told by the local commander, Gruffudd, that they would be separated for their training and induction into the British army, as the juniors would remain at Caerlegeion and the adults would go to Deva. Cadwur argued and remonstrated but to no avail. Gruffudd was the most stubborn man in the land and was adamant that rules were rules and no exception could be made for anyone. The background to this was that the new chief ruler, with his Roman military background, was seeking to run the country on Roman lines with strong central control and rules for all aspects of military affairs clearly set out and written in Latin. This arrangement appealed to Gruffudd, who liked certainty in all aspects of life. He also was aware that in the not too distant past different local rulers had done their own thing and had not always cooperated. This had given an advantage to the Saxons and other enemies.

"If you don't like the rules, you are free to leave and return to your home. Or you may decide to stay here yourself but send your boy home. He looks very young even for a cadet. When your induction has been satisfactorily completed, you will be permitted to see each other and, if the commanders agree, be part of the same militia."

The brave and self-willed Kitto said to his father, "Let us carry on. I can take care of myself and hope that soon we can be together again."

Reluctantly and under protest, Cadwur conceded and then proceeded with the other adults on the journey towards Deva.

Kitto was placed in a group of about twenty cadets based in Caerlegeion under care and tuition of a very experienced commander called Agricola. They were boarded in a military camp to the west of the town adjoining the river. Kitto was rather different from the others in the group and was the only one from Armorica. He was quite tall for his age, but younger than the others, who were from the south of Cambria and from much poorer backgrounds than Kitto. This showed as he wore better clothing, was an excellent rider, could speak and write good Latin, and had detailed knowledge of the New Testament.

---

[80] Caerleon beside the River Usk

During training, Agricola was very impressed with him and saw him as officer material. He also praised him in front of the other boys. This did not go down too well with some of them, particularly with a large and strongly-built lad called Idris. He was from one of the many farming families who had been displaced by settlers from the south of Hibernia. Up to that time no one had come forward to help these farmers to recover their lands. His family had moved to higher but less productive land and had become severely impoverished. There were good reasons why they had sent Idris along to join the army, as he would be paid and would be one less mouth to feed. He had always been treated harshly by his brutal father, who had at times savagely beaten him for the slightest misdemeanour.

With this troubled background, Idris was aggressive and had a serious chip on his shoulder. He and his family also thought that the British soldiers should give priority to driving the Hibernians out of Cambria, as they were a bigger threat than the Saxons.

He and a gang of his followers kept picking on Kitto and harassing him. They would hide away his clothes and kit, and mock the way he spoke. Sometimes they would push him over. There was no serious violence but there was a constant threat of it. The spirited Kitto was getting fed up with this treatment and soon confronted Idris, who said (in Brythonic) with his accustomed aggression, "Are you looking for a fight? Do you want a good hiding?"

Kitto, who had plenty of courage and maturity, said in a confident and grown up way, "I want to talk to you to find out why you all seem to hate me. After all, I came here to help your people defeat the Saxons. I could have stayed in Armorica out of danger, and yet you abuse me."

Kitto, without thinking, spoke these words in good Latin, which came to him more naturally than Brythonic but which Idris could barely understand. Kitto realised his mistake and then said the same thing in Brythonic, which Idris could then clearly understand.

Idris responded in Brythonic, "There you are again showing off how clever you think you are, translating Latin for me. We don't like the way you speak our language with your foreign accent. You think you are superior to us and you are always sucking up to the commander, trying to show us up as inferior. We don't like the way you boast about the wealth of your family and all their money from horse-breeding."

Kitto was dumfounded by these remarks. He had never sought to patronise anyone or to portray himself as superior. He had just told them about his life in Armorica, as he thought they might be interested to know about another land.

He said "Look, Idris, I have no wish to offend you. I speak as I do because I come from Armorica where many people speak both Latin and Brythonic. I was brought up as a Christian and regard all people as equal. I do not regard myself as superior to anyone. I have come here to help the British efforts to drive back the pagan Saxons. I want to be your friend and comrade."

Idris did not respond to logic and politeness but was quick to take offence, giving Kitto a hostile stare. He then threw a punch at him, which Kitto just managed to parry. Idris flew at him and they wrestled to the ground. Idris's gang started cheering and encouraging their leader. The noise came immediately to the attention of an officer, who came in and ordered them to break it up. This was good news for Kitto, as he was not as strong as his unpleasant older opponent and could have been seriously injured, if the fight had gone on much longer.

"What the hell is going on? You two are in dead trouble. The rest of you, move your backsides. Parade is due in a few minutes, when you hear the bugle call, and you'd better be there looking smart."

"You two come with me to the commander, who will not take kindly to your behaviour. The last time this sort of thing happened he was literally speechless with rage."

The commander, Agricola, was indeed very angry. He addressed them in his most stern tones, "I will not tolerate fighting between cadets. If you were not new here or if this was a second offence, I would have both of you soundly thrashed. As it is, you will both be on bread and water for the next two days and have to do fatigues, like cleaning weapons, kitchen pots and pans, and cleaning out the latrines."

He did not ask for any explanation as to whose fault it was that caused them to come to blows, and worked on the assumption that it was six of one and a half dozen of the other. Both boys were very scared of him and did not dare to say anything.

Kitto did not enjoy the next two days but the good thing was that the whole episode had cleared the air and there was no more bullying. Agricola might have had a greater understanding of psychology than was readily obvious from his blunt remarks. Punish everybody and peace will prevail after that!

After the period of punishment, Kitto much enjoyed the training in the fine landscape to the west of the town and particularly liked the river, which he assumed would be home to some fine trout and salmon. Local people caught eels, which were sometimes on the menu for the cadets. They were worked very hard and there was no time for fishing or other leisure pursuits for them.

On one session, they had a long route march to the former Roman fort at Y Gaer[81], which had been a base for Roman cavalry. The cadets were given intensive training in riding horses. This was easy for Kitto, but he took care not to appear much better than the others. Idris fell off a few times, but, although his friends all laughed at him, Kitto did not join in. Idris noticed this and remembered what Kitto had said to him before their fight, about not feeling superior to others. Agricola said to Idris, "Don't worry. Everybody falls off at first; that's how we get to learn."

They remained overnight at Y Gaer, and next day went on a march which took them all the way to the River Honddu, which joined the Uisc in the area known as Brecheiniog.[82] As part of the exercise, the cadets were required to cross the Honddu, where the flowing water was in places up to waist high for them, following a period of wet weather. Two of the cadets slipped on the smooth stones covered in wet mosses on the river bed and fell, with the risk of being washed away in the current. Agricola quickly grabbed one of them and pulled him clear, but did not have time to catch the other. Kitto, a very strong swimmer well taught by his father, had no hesitation and swam in the cold water lifting the other cadet to safety.

The attitude of the cadets towards Kitto changed after this heroic rescue. Whatever his faults might have been, they all felt safer when he was about, as he seemed so capable in all ways.

The arduous training continued for two months and then the cadets were assessed. The best were passed fit to serve in the cavalry; the next category were deemed fit for the infantry; and the less able cadets were designated as camp followers to help with logistics. Kitto was one of the few allocated to the cavalry, and hoped to meet his father again soon. Idris was allocated to the infantry. His strong physique and his aggressive nature, if under control, would surely make him a good foot soldier and a thorn in the side of the Saxons.

---

[81] Near Brecon

[82] This area is Breconshire and was previously known as Garthmadrun, but then named after King Brychen

150

Chapter 34
Army Life in Britannia

Meanwhile, Cadwur and his colleagues, including Matthew, had joined a group of soldiers at the fortress town of Deva. They were subjected to various tests to assess their current level of competence. Cadwur came out well ahead of the others. He was allocated to the cavalry where he was given a role as a trainer in horsemanship and warfare. His expertise in horse-breeding was also noted. He had learnt much of this skill from his father, but would have to confess that he did not have the innate talent of his sister, Nessa, for horse-breeding. He was aware that she had ambitions to be a warrior, and vaguely wondered whether she could ever come to Britannia to advise on horse-breeding. Now he was there, the idea did not seem so farfetched and fanciful as it had seemed in Armorica.

The only induction Cadwur needed was into the administrative procedures of the army and in the signs and signals given, which were not quite the same as those used in Armorica. He was very soon right up to speed.

Gruffudd, whom Cadwur had met in Caerlegeion, was in overall charge of training and was very impressed with Cadwur's skill and commitment.

Matthew also impressed the trainers and assessors. There was little they could teach him about horsemanship or the use of weapons. He learnt, however, about military tactics and the commands and signals which were used.

After two months of training and induction at Deva, Cadwur, Matthew and the others were moved north to Rheged to winter quarters. There Cadwur was allowed to make a start on horse-breeding at a stud farm in that beautiful area of the country with its mountains and large lakes. Whilst missing his family, including the young Kitto, he was in his element in a scenic region and doing what he much enjoyed.

In the spring, Cadwur's group was moved to Luguvalium, a former Roman garrison town situated near the west end of Hadrian's Wall. There he felt honoured and delighted to meet for the first time some horsemen from the Votadini. They and their horses were just as impressive as he had been expecting. One of these warriors, who had the looks and attitude of their leader, was particularly striking and charismatic. He had dark hair and a well-trimmed beard. But his most impressive features were his penetrating brown eyes, which flashed with vitality and panache.

He was introduced to Cadwur and described as the leader of the northern cavalry. He then spoke in a deep and confident voice and said, "My name is Artorius[83]."

Cadwur replied to him, "I am pleased and honoured to meet you, sir. I have heard much of your great skill in leading the cavalry. My name is Cadwur ap Teged of the Conrnovii tribe. I have come here from Trepunek in Armorica to assist as best I can in the struggle against the pagan Saxons, and also to combat the vile Scoti and Picti.

"It has been my dream from an early age to go into combat with the great horsemen of the Votadini and soon this dream will surely come true."

Artorius looked over Cadwur with his keen eyes and was impressed with what he saw. He responded, "I have heard of your prowess in battle and of your great successes in your country. We are heavily indebted to you for making the journey here to assist us in our righteous cause."

Soon after this meeting, there was welcome news for Cadwur, told to him by Gruffudd (in a matter of fact and soldier-like way), "Your son, Kitto, will be joining us next week. The reports say that he has excelled in all his training and has all the makings of a fine cavalry officer."

And so father and son were reunited. They embraced warmly. Cadwur noticed that his son had grown in stature and strength. He was also very self-confident. Having had to stand on his own feet away from family and friends and having had to face adversity had made him grow up very quickly.

Kitto, who was still only thirteen, was made a junior member of the militia in which Artorius and Cadwur were leading officers.

As well as military training and exercises, father and son had time to go hunting together with others in the forests of Rheged and to swim in the cold clear waters of the lakes in this scenic land. When they were together there was

---

[83] This is intended to be the historical character on whom the legendary King Arthur was based.

at times a deep sadness, when they talked about their family, so far away in Armorica.

They both loved Armorica, and one day when they had been talking about home they decided that they would write a letter to Rhian, Cadwur's wife and the mother of young Kitto. They just wanted to let her know that they were well and were in the same militia in the north of Britannia. Cadwur despite his many talents was less skilled in writing Latin than his young son, who had always taken his academic studies as seriously as physical pursuits and military training.

Cadwur dictated what he wanted to say and Kitto carefully wrote it down neatly and in good Latin. He also made some sensible suggestions as they went along, "Perhaps we should not say so much about our razor-sharp swords and spears, our cuirasses and the war leader, Artorius."

"What should we put in instead?"

"We could talk about Rheged and Luguvalium and the lakes and mountains. We have both visited Hadrian's Wall. Mam came from this area and it would be nice for her to hear about it. Mam and grandma would like to know how much we like this area. If we say too much about war and battles, that might make them worry about us."

Cadwur, whose mind was normally on matters military, saw the point and realised how mature his teenage boy was. So he agreed and they then included a current description of Luguvalium, from where Rhian and her family had travelled to Armorica. The letter mentioned in particular that the quarters which had housed the Roman legion there had been restored and enlarged and now accommodated a large and potent British army, including cavalry from the Gododdin.

They put in a paragraph about hunting, swimming and fishing with the implication that they were having a good time and that there was no need to worry.

Whilst composing the letter, they discussed whether at some stage they might go back home on leave, depending on the situation with the Saxons and other enemies. They agreed that they would want to go back at some stage for a visit.

Cadwur thought that they should mention that in the letter as it would cheer up the family, especially Rhian and Sioned.

The ever-thoughtful Kitto was not so sure, "We might raise their hopes and it would be very bad for them if in the end we did not manage to get back home within a year or so. That would make them worry even more."

Again Cadwur saw the point and they did not mention the prospect of a home visit in the letter, as they did not wish to raise hopes which might not in the event be fulfilled.

The letter was completed, signed and sealed and duly dispatched for delivery to Trepunek.

As for Matthew, he was also enjoying his time in Rheged, including the opportunities for hunting and fishing. On a fine spring morning a group from the militia, including Matthew, went off on a hunting expedition in the high ground of the area hoping to catch deer or wild boar. They had with them a fine pack of hounds, full of obvious enthusiasm for the chase. Soon they hunted down and caught a large stag. The animal was no match for the hounds which brought it quickly to the ground to a swift death with sharp teeth in its neck.

Half an hour later after a quiet period in the hunt there was a loud call that there was a massive wild boar in the bracken on the other side of a rough stone wall. Matthew was amongst the first to rush in that direction, but, as his horse landed having jumped the wall, a hoof caught in a deep hole on the far side of the wall and Matthew was thrown to the ground in an awkward fall landing on a jagged stone outcrop. He was in great pain and could not stop himself from yelling out in agony. Colleagues rushed to his help and soon realised that he must have broken his leg. One of the group managed to make a splint from fallen timber and to tie it to his leg. They got him onto a hastily-made stretcher, on which they carried him to the nearest track, to await a carriage to bring him back to the quarters. There his leg received the best treatment available. The broken leg was tied firmly to a proper splint to give it the best chance to heal. He remained in that condition for some weeks, when eventually the splint was removed. Although the leg had healed itself and he was not in any danger, he could only ever walk again with a limp and was deemed not to be fit enough to serve in a cavalry squadron. He therefore decided to go back to his family in Armorica. This all happened after Cadwur's letter had already been sent on its way to Trepunek. Otherwise the news of the accident and intended return could have been sent for onward transmission to his family at Condate.

After a long and stormy sea voyage and then a short and uncomfortable journey over land, Matthew finally got home to his family. Morwenna was more than delighted to see him and held him tenderly in her arms. At the same time, she was worried about his leg and was sad to see the man she loved so much limping and in some pain. That night when they were in bed, she showed him how much she had missed him and how very much she loved him. When their sweet love had taken its course, they spoke together about their future. Matthew reassured her that there were still many things he could do in the home and on the farm. He said that he expected his leg to improve in time as the injury was still quite recent and he had also had to cope with a long and uncomfortable sea voyage. He also told her many things about his time in Britannia until his eyes had to close and deep sleep stopped him saying any more as the loving couple lay together.

Chapter 35
Active Service in Britannia

It was as well that Cadwur had not talked in the letter about coming home. In the summer of 483, any thoughts of home for Cadwur and his son were dashed, as news reports came in that a new wave of Saxons had arrived in the north of the country, leading to an army amassing near the border between the land held by the Saxons and that still under British control. Reconnaissance was carried out, and the advice to the commanders was that it was an infantry army of about one thousand men. It was not known how they were armed but it was assumed that they would have bows and arrows, javelins, swords and the usual fearsome Saxon battle-axes. It was understood that they would have the support of a detachment of charioteers.

A contingent of cavalry to be led by Artorius, plus some infantry, was assembled to confront the new Saxon threat. Cadwur was part of the cavalry with the command of the left wing. Kitto was deemed to be too young for involvement in this battle and remained in the stables, helping with the horses.

The strategy and tactics were worked out in meticulous detail. The cavalry would conceal its self as best it could in higher ground on the British side of the divide, and a small group of infantry would cross over to the Saxon side to tempt the Saxons into confronting them. The Saxons would be expected to take the bait and then chase them over to the British territory, where the Saxons would be met by the cavalry, who would both protect their own infantry and also attack the Saxons.

As often happened, on the night before a battle, Cadwur would have a dream of a victory and the glory that went with it. This occasion was no exception. As always Cadwur slept soundly and this time had a dream about routing the enemy on the battlefield.

They all rose early next morning and prepared for battle. The British army got themselves into their positions, with Cadwur feeling supremely confident, not least because he was so impressed in every way with their leader, Artorius.

The time came for action and the plan was followed to the letter. As expected the Saxons were drawn into the trap of entering the British territory to be faced by the cavalry on the higher ground. The central squadron of the cavalry charged first, leading to fierce fighting. The Saxons put up firm resistance but were no match for the cavalry led by the mighty Artorius. Then the two wings of the cavalry moved in upon the flanks of the Saxon force, and a massacre of Saxons ensued. Cadwur played his part with his usual vigour and panache, but he soon realised that he was far inferior to Artorius, who seemed to have superhuman powers. This Celtic warrior made Cadwur think of the heroes he had been told about in classical epic poems. Artorius' prowess called to mind Achilles and Hector. The monk under whom he had studied at Ponterle had read to the class from an abbreviated Latin translation of the Iliad, which made a deep impression on the young Cadwur.

Cadwur had been told that Artorius was of noble Roman and Votadini descent and this clearly showed in his skill in the arts of war. The ferocity of his attacks on the enemy and the number he slew on his own were awesome to observe, even for a seasoned warrior like Cadwur.

After the battle the surviving Saxons were put to flight, including those of their charioteers who had survived, whilst many of their colleagues lay dead or seriously wounded on the field of battle. That day there were many new widows and orphans and much lamentation in the Saxon lands. At the same time, there were thoughts of revenge against the British forces. Some older Saxons prayed to their God of War for the total defeat of the British.

From the dead and wounded, the British infantry collected as many weapons as they could, particularly the fearsome battle-axes, which they themselves would put to good use in subsequent battles or skirmishes. They also took armour and helmets from dead bodies. The British did not intervene at dusk when the Saxons removed their dead for burial.

Over the next two years there were some more similar battles along the frontier between the two peoples. In each case, the British force led by Artorius were successful in holding back the Saxons. Cadwur continued to lead a wing of the cavalry with distinction and was duly praised by the commanders of British forces. He got to know the commander of the other wing of the cavalry, a member of a noble family of the Votadini. His name was Bedwyr. He and Cadwur often met to chat and drink wine. Kitto sometimes joined them. On one occasion, Bedwyr mentioned Cunedda[84], a noble warrior of the Votadini.

"I have heard the name from my uncle Maldwyn, who knows all about British history, but I cannot recall why this warrior is famous," said Cadwur.

Kitto joined in, "I think he became the king of the north of Cambria about fifty years ago."

Bedwyr responded, "That is correct, Kitto. You are well informed. The British nobles of that area asked for help from the Votadini in expelling Hibernian settlers from their coastal areas. A branch of the Votadini, headed by Cunedda went there in the early part of this century, and they drove many of these settlers out of the coastal areas, including from the Isle of Mona[85]. Cunedda was later accepted by the nobles and people as their king of the north of Cambria.

"I am related to him as my grandfather was a second cousin of his but my part of the Votadini did not join Cunedda in his venture. I am told that subsequent kings and rulers of most parts of Cambria claim kinship with or descent from Cunedda."

Kitto asked for clarification as to whether these Hibernians were the same as the Scoti.

Bedwyr replied, "No, young Kitto, they were from the southern half of Hibernia and their wish was to settle in Britannia and take land, rather than to carry out pillaging raids like the Scoti, who are from the north of Hibernia. My grandfather told me that the British Bishop Patrick was sent to Hibernia, not only to convert the population to Christianity, but also in the hope of dissuading them from migrating to Britannia as pirates or settlers."

Cadwur replied, "This would not be surprising since, as from the fall of the Roman Empire, the Catholic Church seems to use its influence to secure worthy objectives of a temporal nature as well as spreading the Christian message."

Kitto then remembered the cadet Idris, whose family had been displaced by Hibernians in Menevia. He did not say anything as he had not told his father of the bullying.

---

[84] This historical figure's English name is Kenneth. It is believed that the above information about him is substantially correct.
[85] Anglesey. Ynys Môn in Brythonic and Welsh

Chapter 36
Trouble with the Picti

Something unexpected occurred in the year 484 involving the Picti, who had not caused any serious problems for a few years. The Selgovae were one of the tribes in the Gododdin, who had been loyal to the Romans and later to the Britons. In that year, there had been a serious and acrimonious dispute within that tribe. This led a small and disaffected group from the tribe to enter into discussion with some of those Picti, who had been allowed to remain in the Gododdin as peaceful settlers. The disaffected Selgovae hoped that these Picti might help them to gain supremacy within their tribe and enable them to gain vengeance on the majority of the tribe who had opposed them. It was a sort of civil war within a tribe and anything could happen.

Things soon did indeed happen and did so in a complicated way. The Gododdin Picti unexpectedly enlisted support from various kinsfolk living north of the Antonine Wall. These more warlike northern Picti had their own agenda, which was to take the easy opportunity on offer of getting into the land south of Hadrian's Wall to carry out raids in Rheged or north-east Britain, by means of an overland route rather than by sea which could be more hazardous. They planned to achieve this by travelling through the land belonging to the disaffected Selgovae, which should be an open door for them.

This strategy was successful for them and soon led to several serious Pictish raids into Rheged by a large hoard of Picti and several members of the Selgovae tribe who were dragged along by a momentum which they had not intended or foreseen. These dissident Selgovae had been hoodwinked by the more cunning and ruthless Picti.

There were reports of pillage and rape, and of the abduction of British people into slavery. The situation was very serious and urgent and effective action was needed.

This all took place when Artorius and the chief ruler were in Glevum, many miles from Rheged. It fell to Cadwur and Bedwyr to assemble a fighting force to address this menace. A main army from Luguvalium headed by Cadwur soon faced a Pictish and Selgovae force near to the city and routed them. Few of the Picti and Selgovae survived. But that was only the start of the solution. There were numerous bands of Picti and some of the Selgovae in the more remote parts of the land causing havoc to the local population. The only solution was the formation of small militias to patrol as much land as possible and to confront the invaders soon as any were discovered.

This well-tried strategy, which had been used by the Romans in the past, was put into practice again. The youthful Kitto, who had not so far been involved in active service, was given a senior role in one of these militias and soon justified his position. His militia fell upon a band of blood-thirsty Picti rampaging in villages and farms near one of the large lakes. They were stopped in their tracks by accurate and deadly javelins thrown with great skill by Kitto and his men. The invaders, having sustained losses tried to escape, were cut off by a small squadron of cavalry which had surrounded them and prevented their escape. They were slaughtered to a man and their Pictish blood stained the good earth of Rheged and may even have enriched its soil near those villages.

In this way, the invasion was soundly defeated. When the news of these events came to Artorius and to the chief ruler, they were delighted and proud of the efforts made by the militias led and organised by Cadwur. They noted the great achievements of the young Armorican, Kitto, in particular his outstanding skills with the javelin.

Some of the leading members of the Selgovae tribe were captured and transported back to the Gododdin, where they were summarily executed.

The leaders of the Votadini called a meeting of all the tribes of the Gododdin to confirm their policy of keeping the Picti to the north of the Antonine Wall other than those who wished to live peacefully within the Gododdin. This policy held sway for a generation and all warlike Picti were kept out of the Gododdin.

At this time there were also a few sea-borne raids by the Scoti, along the coasts of Rheged, but these were repulsed by the British forces. It seems that such raids were less frequent or effective since the mission by Bishop Patrick to Hibernia to convert the people there to the true Faith and to the ways of peace.

Such raids were now seen as a minor irritant, as compared to what they had been in the past and in comparison with the long-term threat from the Saxons.

Chapter 37
The Warriors on Leave

Cadwur continued as a commander in the cavalry based in Rheged, as well as assisting with the breeding of horses, for another two years. Things had calmed down on the frontier with the Saxons over this period, and Cadwur's request to return to Armorica with his son for a period of leave was granted. And so in the year 485, father and son made the long journey by sea to their home port of Tregaran. After this long voyage, they arrived safely and were delighted to be united with their family at Trepunek.

But the joy of their return was tempered by the very sad news that Sioned, the mother of Cadwur, had died earlier that year. Her husband, Teged, was now elderly and desperately missed his dear wife, as did their children and grandchildren. It was a great relief to see Cadwur and Kitto again, as there was every fear that they could be killed in battle. Rhian had also missed her husband. They were still very much in love with each other. She hugged Cadwur and then, having kissed her son, said, "How you have grown, dear Kitto! You are no longer the young boy who left us, but have returned as a young soldier. Although I did not want you to leave us, I knew that you had set your heart on doing so and I am very proud of you. I am so glad that you have spent time in the lovely part of Britannia where I and my family came from."

Cadwur also hugged his son and said, "Kitto has performed with great distinction and has gained the praise of the military trainers and the commanders in the north of Britannia."

Their safe return was a truly joyful and unexpected event. In a few days' time, there was a lavish celebration with banquet, carousing and dancing. Matthew already back from Britannia, with Morwenna and their family, readily accepted the invitation to join in. Young Luke, Kitto's childhood friend, came along with his parents. He was now a member of the militia based at Condate.

Nessa was delighted to see her brother and her nephew, but was also keen to ask about horse-breeding in Rheged. She had still retained her dream of being involved in some way in warfare.

Kitto and Luke were pleased to have the chance to talk to each other about their experiences in recent years. Luke was impressed with all the military activity of his friend. He too had stories to tell as he was by then a member of the cavalry in the militia. The two young men also reminisced about their childhood exploits, including the attempted abduction and their practice with archery and with javelin throwing. Kitto said that his long years of practice with the javelin had paid off, in the battles and skirmishes in which he had participated.

By this time, Nessa and her husband, with some help from Teged, were excelling at horse-breeding, and were becoming ever more famous at this skill. They had sold horses to most of the militias in Armorica, as well as to farmers. With permission from the local ruler they had sold some heavy horses to the Franks, in the vicinity of Condate. Christianity was spreading amongst the Franks by this time, and perhaps it was for this reason that there was less of a threat from them towards the Armoricans, who were seen as peaceful people.

Nessa had by now bred many fine horses but she was most proud of a grey colt that she and Medar had produced two years earlier. He was fast, strong, brave and very responsive to a good rider. She knew her animals and was convinced that he had the potential to be the best warhorse ever to come from Armorica. The elderly Teged was inclined to agree with her and was increasingly impressed with the skill of his daughter. He thought, *what a son and grandson I have, the bravest of warriors, but what a daughter: not only can she find treasure but also breed the best horses.*

In the following week, Cadwur rode the colt and agreed that Nessa was not exaggerating the colt's potential. Nessa did not want him gelded but thought he should be allowed to grow to a stallion and used for breeding. Cadwur readily concurred that he should never be gelded, but thought that the emphasis should be on his future as a horse for the cavalry. The family realised that he needed a suitable name. After long discussion of classical and Celtic names, they agreed on 'Cedewain', which was a part of Powys much loved by Teged and his late brother Owain.

Chapter 38
Return to Britannia

In the Year of our Lord 487, word came to Armorica that the Britons were planning a new major campaign against the Saxons, and Cadwur got to hear of it. Whilst he enjoyed the peaceful life in Armorica, especially the hunting in the woods and forests, he was a warrior at heart and felt an overwhelming urge to go back to Britannia for the campaign against the Saxons. Kitto, who was now seventeen, shared his father's enthusiasm.

No one in the family wanted them to go and risk their precious lives, but they feared that their pleas would fall in deaf ears. They were quite right about that, as it was obvious to all that Cadwur and Kitto were determined to go back to Britannia.

But there were two other persons who were keen to join them. One was Nessa. She wanted to go back across the sea to help with horse-breeding and the care of warhorses. She spoke to Cadwur, her brother, "I know you and Dad have always said that there is no place in warfare for women. I accept that they cannot join in battles, but there is so much more to be done when there are battles, like preparing and caring for the horses. That is something which I am very used to doing. I should like to join you in the journey to Britannia and Medar also wishes to come with us. We could bring some fine horses with us, including Cedewain, if you agree, perhaps even to offer him to Artorius for his cavalry squadron."

Cadwur was taken aback by this bold suggestion, and paused for a while to think about it. He knew that there was always a need for good horses over there, with some inevitable losses in battle and in intense training. He was wondering what Artorius would say if he were to see Cedewain and some of the other fine horses from the family's stud. They were at least a match for those of the Votadini.

The very next day, he spoke to his sister and her husband, more in the manner of a military commander than a relative, "Nessa, I have thought about your proposal to accompany us with horses, and I am inclined to give my consent. I am sure that these fine horses would be welcome there and you and Medar would need to be with them to get them settled in their new surroundings. As you have said, you and indeed Medar could perform a useful role in tending to horses and perhaps in helping and advising about breeding. Good horses are crucial in warfare. Your skill and experience would surely give us an advantage over the enemy.

"Medar, are you also fully committed to going with us?"

"Yes indeed. I have heard so much about that country and would love to go there and assist with the war effort. I would really like to go as far as Rheged and see those mountains and large lakes. I have heard so much about them from our family. I should also like to see the famous Hadrian's Wall."

Nessa was delighted with the sentiments of her brother and the support of her husband and relished the challenges ahead.

Thus it was settled. Teged was not too happy. He feared that he might lose more than just Cadwur and Kitto, but there was a powerful tide running and he knew he could not hold it back.

The other person who wanted to travel to Britannia with them was the young Luke. His request was firmly vetoed by both his parents. Matthew made the crucial point that he would have to be trained and inducted into the British army, which would take weeks and he may not be ready by the time of the forthcoming campaign. With some reluctance, Luke decided not to continue with his request to travel.

The following year a sizeable group from Armorica, including Cadwur, Kitto, Nessa and Medar, set sail from Tregaran, with horses and weapons of war on their journey to Dumnonia. From there they travelled over land to Glevum, where they were greeted and warmly welcomed by the British nobility, including Artorius, who was visiting that city together with his wife, Gwenllian. Cadwur introduced his sister and her husband to Artorius.

"As you know, Artorius, my father was a famous breeder of fine horses both here and in Armorica. This activity has been carried on by my sister, Nessa, and her husband, Medar. They are now with us to help in the care of horses and to assist with horse-breeding if that should be required. Dear leader, Artorius, Nessa has something to say to you."

Nessa then bowed to Artorius and said, "Sir, if you would like to accompany us to the stables, I have a fine stallion there to show you."

"Gentle lady, I should be pleased to do so."

The group of them went over to the stables, where Nessa showed the excellent Cedewain to Artorius and his companions. She said with due respect and modesty, "This stallion is called Cedewain, and he is one of the finest we have ever produced. He loves being ridden fast. He is brave and very sure-footed. He has an excellent pedigree for a warhorse. My family would like to offer him to you and would be most honoured if you would accept him as our gift."

Artorius was initially lost for words, as he was overwhelmed by the sight of this wonderful horse and by the generosity of Cadwur and his highly talented family. Whilst he was trying to find words to express his deep emotions, his wife, Gwenllian, who had joined the others, spoke for herself and on his behalf, "Madam, he is the most beautiful horse I have ever seen, and I would really like to ride this gorgeous creature myself, if I ever get the chance. It is rare for Artorius to be lost for words, but we can understand how emotional he feels having received such a generous offer."

Then Artorius cleared his throat and responded, "Thank you so much, dear lady. This is a most generous and wonderful gift which I am more than delighted to accept. You and your husband are most welcome here. Cadwur should be very proud of you both."

Nessa smiled with obvious pleasure and added in modest and respectful tones, "He is an entire horse and can be used for breeding apart from any other duties."

Chapter 39
The Beauty of Gwenllian

Cadwur, who loved his wife dearly and was devoted to her and his family, could not help noticing how beautiful Gwenllian was. She looked much younger than Artorius and was said to be the most beautiful lady in the whole of Britannia. When Cadwur and Nessa were introduced to her, Gwenllian was wearing a long gown in the finest velvet in the colour burgundy. It fitted her perfectly and showed off her curvaceous figure. She also wore magnificent Celtic jewellery. She had luxuriant long dark hair and lovely light brown eyes. Her complexion was perfect. Her posture and decorum showed that she was of noble birth, and her voice was clear, mellow and seductive. They were told that she was also an accomplished singer and lyre player. Cadwur could well believe that she would have a beautiful singing voice. When she moved, it was with a grace and elegance beyond compare.

Gwenllian was only eighteen when Artorius had fallen madly in love with her. At the time, he was already a distinguished warrior aged thirty. Early in their marriage they had a child, a healthy boy, but no other children followed. There was speculation that Artorius had suffered a war wound, which had the effect of preventing him fathering any more children.[86] This was just a rumour and there was no direct evidence to support it.

As time went by Artorius was promoted to a higher military rank, and this meant that he was often away from home for long periods of time, whether fighting battles or training and organising the cavalry and other forces. When he returned to their castle, Gwenllian was delighted to see him and wanted him to make love to her. Often he was too fatigued to oblige by the rigours of battles and by long journeys over roads in dilapidated condition. Whilst fondly

---

[86] This is entirely fictional, but a respectful gesture towards the legend of the Fisher King

sympathising with his weariness, she felt in her heart that he should want to perform his duty as a husband. The thought crossed her mind that he may no longer be as virile as when he was younger.

Gwenllian might have been lonely in his absence, but for her two younger sisters who lived in the castle with her and acted as her ladies-in-waiting. Her childhood nurse also resided in the castle and performed the role of her housekeeper and chambermaid.

There were rumours (no more than that) to the effect that she had taken lovers[87] when her husband was away. Her entourage were absolutely loyal to her and totally discrete. If there were clandestine meetings, none of them ever spoke of it, out of respect for her and in fear of what might happen if Artorius ever got to hear such rumours. He was held in such high esteem that the most important of the Britons could not bring themselves to believe anything less than good about him or his wife.

As Cadwur said his farewells to Artorius and to Gwenllian, he acknowledged to himself that if he were ever alone with her he might be tempted to feelings and actions which he could not control, such was her stunning beauty. He was soon to be heavily engaged in military preparations and thereafter any thoughts of Gwenllian were no longer in the forefront of his mind.

---

[87] In the Arthurian myths, his queen had a lover, Lancelot. Perhaps a similar situation existed for the historical Arthur.

Chapter 40
Warhorse

For Artorius and his colleagues, the next few months in the year 488 were spent preparing for and planning the campaign to drive back the Saxons. In the meantime, there were several skirmishes, but no real battles. Artorius, Cadwur, and Kitto, along with Nessa and Medar, had moved to the scenic region of Rheged. Some of the horses from Armorica were there with them, including Cedewain. When they first arrived, Nessa rode him to show Artorius just how fast he could go and how responsive he was to his rider. It was a magnificent sight observing horse and rider in perfect harmony speeding through the fine countryside.

Artorius was surprised and impressed to see a lady so skilfully riding such a large and powerful stallion and at high speed. He concluded correctly that horsemanship was in her blood, as well as horse-breeding.

Artorius, a most excellent rider, was able to establish an immediate rapport with a horse. He mounted Cedewain and could not fail to notice how responsive he was to his rider. He was also aware of the power and speed of the young stallion. He rode the horse at speed but deliberately for his first ride did not try to emulate the speed achieved by the highly talented Nessa.

The horse, having been well trained and exercised in Armorica and later in Britannia, was exceptionally muscular for his age. Artorius guessed that he must be about fifteen hands, a very suitable size for a warhorse.

He said to Cadwur, "This horse which your most excellent sister has bred is quite magnificent. The best young warhorse I have ever seen. When the time comes, I should like to ride him into battle myself, and I hope that you and your sister would be content for me to do that."

Cadwur was much flattered by Artorius' assessment of the stallion. Responding with great respect to Artorius, he said, "We should be greatly honoured if you were to ride him into battle but is there not a great risk for a leader to ride a grey? It would seem perhaps to be an easy target for the enemy?"

"That is a fair point in the case of most riders, but I win battles by boldness. I want the enemy to know that it is I who am leading the charge. I want to put the fear of God into them from the very first moment of the conflict. If word gets around that I am riding a grey, so be it. My boldness and determination is why the chief ruler has now designated me as Dux Bellorum. [88] In Cedewain, I would have a mou of the utmost boldness matching my own."

---

[88] Leader (or Duke) of Battles. Some traditions say that this was Arthur's title.

Chapter 41
The Great Battle

To the east of Rheged, there was a range of tall hills, separating the lands still under British control from the regions occupied by those Saxons known as the Angles. The most important of these hills was Badon Hill, a round-shaped hill with gentle slopes, and containing some upland pastures and some broad-leafed woods. In times of peace, it was home to flocks of sheep and provided a location for a happy day of hunting in its woods. There was also scope for collecting nuts and a range of mushrooms. On its favoured south side there were some old orchards, which still produced fine fruit in a good year. With the invasions and migrations of recent years, this hill was seen as a strategic location which the Britons were committed to holding on to.

And so Badon Hill was now occupied by British infantry, in view of its important location, but under constant attack or threat of attack from the Saxons, who saw it as a gateway to the British lands to the west. In their strange Germanic language, we are told that they called the large region of Britannia to the west of this hill 'the District of the Lakes', which was an accurate (if rather prosaic) description of the area. They too realised that whoever held Badon Hill would have a major strategic advantage.

In late spring of the year 490, word came that there was a Saxon army amassing on the territory to the east side of Badon Hill. The intelligence was conflicted to some extent, particularly as to numbers and about the type of forces. The consensus view was that there was a sizeable force with infantry and charioteers, but probably little or no cavalry. Artorius took in all the information available and thought over how best to meet this challenge, both in terms of resources and timing. After much thought, he called together his commanders and other senior warriors, who included Cadwur and Bedwyr.

Artorius then addressed them in a formal but friendly way, speaking in his well-recognised deep and rather lyrical voice. He spoke in Latin in its dialect common in the north of Britannia, "Gentlemen, friends, fellow-warriors, and followers of the true Faith, we now face a new challenge in the form of this large Saxon army some distance to the east of Badon Hill. We cannot be sure of numbers or of how many of them are seasoned warriors as opposed to farmers with spears. We estimate that we will be outnumbered but will have a big advantage in cavalry and chariots.

"We have been victorious in many battles along the frontier with the heathen Saxons, but we now need to prepare for what may turn out to be the most crucial battle of all. The objective is to hold on to Badon Hill and it surrounding fields on all sides and to dissuade the enemy from ever trying to capture it again.

"We know that more and more heathen Saxons are invading our precious island. Some just want to farm the land which was allocated to them in the past, but others are predatory and warlike, wishing to push us ever further to the west. In the past our leaders unwisely thought that we could live in peace with the Saxon migrants, but recent history has taught us that they pose a real threat to our very existence on this fairest isle of ours.

"We must, dear friends, and we *will* fight with all our might and main to retain what we have, including the scenic lands of Rheged. Badon Hill is vital to our survival.

"We must expect the Saxons to be well-armed and more numerous than us, and we know only too well that they have inflicted injury on us with their crude battle-axes. But they have never been a match for our cavalry and our well-trained infantry. We must not forget our charioteers, who have always got the better of their counterparts in the Saxon army. We have a proud heritage in warfare of all kinds having fought many battles on our own account and in the past as federates of the great Roman legions. We have learnt much from our forefathers and from the great Roman generals, whom we have supported. I will now give you my proposals for my strategy in the battle soon to come, and would welcome your views."

There was a respectful silence when he had paused. No-one uttered a single word, but there were clear and obvious signs of total approval to the sentiments expressed by the Dux Bellorum from the military commanders. He had put their very thoughts into his own elegant and powerful language.

Artorius explained in minute detail his plan for the battle, which he then discussed with his colleagues, taking in some of their suggestions and giving clarification where needed.

Reliable information then came in that the Saxons were on the move in the direction of Badon Hill. Artorius decided that the time to take action had arrived a little sooner than expected.

The chosen day for the battle therefore was upon them. As always on the eve of a battle, Cadwur slept soundly and had a dream about the forthcoming encounter. Whilst on this occasion he dreamt of victory, he saw the body of a British soldier lying immobile on the battlefield. The body seemed familiar. Cadwur awoke in a sudden jolt believing that the body was that of his son, Kitto. When he came to himself, his first thought was to urge Kitto to withdraw from the battle, but he decided not to do so. He knew how strong-willed his son was and that he would insist upon going into his first major battle, for which he had been preparing for years. Cadwur thought that, if he asked Kitto not to participate, his son would carry on regardless but may have his confidence affected by his father's misgivings. And so matters proceeded as planned.

For everyone, there was the usual mixture of emotions just before a battle; everything from excitement, the desire for a swift victory, the quest for glory, but at the same time, from knowledge that there are always uncertainties in war, a general sense of unease together with a wish to get started. As has often been said in times of war, the waiting is the worst part. It affected different warriors in different ways. Those who had fought many battles before handled the waiting well and were able to clear their minds of negative thoughts and focus on the task ahead. Some of the inexperienced fighters could not control their feelings in the same way but at the same time felt confidence seeing their valiant war leader. Kitto was particularly excited and felt confident.

The mixture of feelings may well have been the same on the Saxon side, under the leadership of a youthful noble warrior called Oswy. It was not known in Britannia that he and his ancestors claimed descent from the Norse God of Thunder, Thor. On the eve of battle, the Saxons were led in prayer to their gods by their elders, who then made their customary sacrifices.

On the British side the Eucharist had been celebrated in churches throughout Rheged, followed by special prayers for the valiant British military forces in their campaign against the heathen Saxons.

In the early morning of the battle, the weather had been fine but cold. The great Artorius and his army had arisen at dawn, to clad themselves in their battle dress and armour and to take up their razor-sharp weapons. The warhorses had been made ready for action by the stable hands. Nessa, filled with anxiety but also with determination to do her duty, took great care to saddle up and prepare Cedewain for the day ahead, as the mount of Artorius. This was a great honour for her, and she knew that her father Teged would share her pride. She knew that this great stallion was fully in tune with all the enthusiasm and boldness of the cavaliers. She recognised in him that morning all the excitement and sense of adventure which she had seen so often in him. He was raring to go, but would always follow the directions of his famous rider.

Artorius was an awesome figure astride this fine grey stallion, a mount which fully matched the intensity and authority of the Dux Bellorum. As he moved forward, he was joined on either side by his customary standard-bearers, proud men of noble birth and battle-hardened with the scars to show for it. The Saxons would know without doubt who was leading the cavalry charge against them. There was no doubt that this would put fear into their hearts.

There was amongst the British a young rider, who was overwhelmingly excited and proud to be part of this prestigious cavalry force. This was Kitto, now a man of twenty years, powerfully built and bearded. He had fought well in several conflicts and skirmishes already, but never in a major battle. Now he was eagerly expecting to play a part in the most significant battle for a generation. He hoped that his would be a major part.

Cadwur and Bedwyr, each commanding a wing of the cavalry, were astride their horses and had all the aura of fearsome warriors.

And so it was that the two armies came together to do battle in the early morning of that day. It was gradually getting warmer but was cloudy and overcast, with the effect that neither side would be at a disadvantage from having the bright rising sun in their eyes as they faced their enemy.

Artorius led the cavalry charge into the Saxon lines with his usual power and fury. He resembled a wrathful and hungry wolf attacking a vast flock of mountain sheep. Although the Saxons fought bravely, including their leader Oswy, they were no match for the British cavalry. Artorius slew so many of them with his mighty sword called 'Caliburn' that eye-witnesses swore that the friction of severing so many Saxon limbs and bones had caused Caliburn to become red-hot and give off smoke.

Cadwur also fought in his usual bold and effective way, and he too killed many Saxons on that famous day. He suffered a few flesh wounds but his reactions were too fast for his enemies to do him any real harm. He was glad that his reactions had not slowed down greatly now that he was getting older. Although he was not as swift in thought and action as a young man, he made up for any shortfall by his long experience in battle, and his great skill as a horseman.

The din of the battle was awesome and terrifying, especially to those engaged in battle for the first time. There were the strident bugle calls, the shouts from the leaders, the clash of steel on steel, the thunderous hooves of the horses, the unearthly screams of the wounded and the dying. All this noise disturbed and upset the wildlife of the area, except for the carrion crows, to which a battle was a promising event with the prospect of humans offering their flesh in abundance to these ever hungry scavenging birds.

The battle continued for hours, often with small battles within the main contest. By early afternoon, the British had again routed the Saxons, and those enemy soldiers who were still alive and mobile had run away as fast as they could, except for a few brave souls who remained to the bitter end hoping for help from Thor. These included the Saxon leader, the brave Oswy, who remained in his chariot. It was not in his noble nature to run away or to surrender, whatever the odds. Oswy and the few Saxons hid behind a coppice and waited. Was Thor going to answer their prayers?

Then one of those rare freak events which occasionally happen in warfare occurred (whether by pure chance or divine intervention). A single arrow from a Saxon bow shot at random in the direction of the victorious cavalry struck Artorius' steed, Cedewain, in the eye with such force that it pierced the animal's brain. The brave horse reared up in shock and agony and threw off Artorius, who dropped to the ground in a heavy and awkward fall. He had let go of his sword Caliburn as he hit the ground and, weighed down by his heavy armour, struggled unsuccessfully to get up and retake his mighty weapon.

The group of valiant Saxons (but not at that time Oswy) saw what had happened and, leaving their hiding place, ran towards Artorius, eager to kill the champion of their foe and to take some revenge for the loss of so many of their compatriots. As it happened there were few Britons near to their leader, as it seemed to all that the battle had already been won, but Cadwur, who was the nearest, observed Artorius' plight and rushed to his aid with lightning speed.

With fire and anger in his eyes, he dispatched all those Saxons with single sword thrusts. It seemed that Artorius was saved.

But it was not only Cadwur who witnessed Artorius' fall. Oswy, the Saxon commander, who had laid in wait, also saw what was happening. Then like a cunning fox, he made his move. In an instant he bravely rushed to the scene to kill Artorius and his rescuer, and thereby at least take something of great value from the Saxon defeat.

Cadwur was so intent on saving Artorius, and then trying to get him back on to his feet, that he did not see Oswy arriving on the scene. Cadwur was too slow to react to the sudden attack which came from Oswy, who was moving fast towards the fallen Artorius in his chariot. The Saxon leader struck Cadwur across the neck with his sword, severing his jugular vein, and causing him to fall to the ground, losing consciousness.

Oswy then alighted from his chariot and paused to give all his attention to the much-hated Artorius, responsible for so many of the deaths of his fellow men. "Artorius", he said loudly in his Germanic language, "Your time has come, you slayer of the Saxons."

With his sword at the ready, he prepared to perform the coup de grace.

Then it was that the young and courageous Kitto, who had already dismounted from his horse, saw to his horror what had been unfolding. He was about forty yards away from his father and Artorius. He assessed the situation very quickly, and realised that he would not have time to mount his horse and ride over to the scene. He grabbed his trusty javelin. He knew he had only one chance and that his throw had to be absolutely accurate. He took aim and threw the sharp weapon with great force. It rose up in an arc, descended at speed, and struck the brave Oswy in the breast at his left nipple going straight into his noble heart. He fell dead instantly and the Saxon threat was over. All the practice at javelin throwing which he had carried out over so many years of his young life together with his steely concentration gave him the consummate skill needed to save the great war leader.

Kitto rushed to his fallen father, who was still alive but fading fast. Cadwur spoke, "Well done, my darling son. I saw what you did and I am so proud of you. My reactions were too slow. This sort of warfare is for younger men. We have between us saved the life of the great Artorius, who will be famous for ever in song and story. You have done enough, my dear son. Go back to peaceful

Armorica and care for your mother and your family, who love you so dearly and never wanted you to join me here."

"You are the best father in the world and have always been my hero. You too saved the life of our great leader."

Cadwur thought of his dream. *The dead soldier was not my son but myself, whom I always thought to be indestructible.*

Kitto wanted to say more, but it was too late. The great Cadwur asked for God's mercy and then gave up his soul. Kitto was utterly shaken. His first experience of a major battle contained all the elements of warfare: honour, glory, courage, skill with weapons and tactics, but more than anything loss and grief much too hard for a young soldier to bear.

Artorius was now being supported by other members of the cavalry, who arrived on the scene, having witness these unforeseen events. At last, he was able to stand. He came over to Kitto and to the body of Cadwur. Artorius wept. He was lost for words at this tragic sight.

Then after a few moments to compose himself, he spoke in his deep and resonant voice, this time speaking more poignantly in the British language, "This battle has taken away the greatest hero of Armorica, who came here of his own volition to assist us in our time of need, and who has always fought more valiantly than anyone. He gave up his life defending me from immediate death. But he did even more than that. He brought his wonderful son with him and it was this most brave and excellent young man who finally saved my life."

Kitto was too traumatised to say anything, but was beginning to realise the enormity of the events which had transpired at the end of this battle. He had saved the great war leader but lost his own father. Kitto wept bitterly.

The fine stallion, Cedewain, lay dead on the battlefield, along with many other horses and warriors.

Chapter 42
The Song of Cadwur

The news of these events spread rapidly in Britannia and came to the ears of the chief ruler, Ambrosius Aurelianus, who was proud of and most grateful for the decisive victory, but bitterly sad at the loss of Cadwur, who had given his life to save the great Artorius.

Gwenllian, the wife of Artorius, wept at the news of the death of Cadwur. She was also greatly distressed at the loss of the fine stallion from Armorica, which sadly she would never have the chance to ride.

A week later at the imposing church at Luguvalium, Cadwur's funeral service took place. The fine building (formerly a Temple to Ceres) was packed with mourners. Cadwur's only relatives able to attend were Kitto, Nessa and Medar. They took comfort from the presence of the chief ruler, Ambrosius Aurelianus, along with many British nobles and, of course, Artorius, who all came to pay their respects to a great hero. Artorius gave a long and touching eulogy for a man who had saved his life and for whom he had the utmost respect.

After the service a large and powerful infantryman made his way over to the main mourners, and asked whether he might have a word with Kitto. His name was Idris and he had been a defender of Badon Hill and had participated in the great battle leading a cohort of infantry with great valour. He said to Kitto, "Dear Kitto, you might remember me. I am Idris, the young cadet from Cambria, who was horrible to you and abused you when we were both training at Caerlegeion. I soon realised what a brave bloke you were and I am not surprised to learn of your crucial contribution in that fierce battle in which we both participated. Idris spoke these heart-felt words in Latin, which he had been required to learn to higher standard, in order to be promoted in the army. You have my deepest sympathy for the loss of your dear father. You and he are truly great heroes."

Kitto was very touched and lost for words. The two men embraced, both overcome with emotion.

They then proceeded to the burial at the cemetery on the edge of the city.

Cadwur was buried there with full military honours.

A further honour was afforded to Cadwur by Ambrosius Aemilianus, who directed that a poem should be composed for him by a bard, in accordance with the best Celtic traditions. This duty fell upon Dwyryd, the most distinguished bard in the land. Kitto took on the task of writing a long and full obituary for his dear father. The young man was scholarly, as well as being a warrior, and performed this duty by writing a full and excellent tribute in good Latin. It was a sad duty for him, and his aunt Nessa supported and assisted him. As well as reminding him of a few details in his father's life and career, she embraced him and wiped away his tears as he continued and completed his serious task.

His work was passed over to Dwyryd, who was multi-lingual, speaking and able to read and write in both Latin and Brythonic, as well as the rather different Celtic tongue spoken by the peoples of Hibernia.[89] And so, he composed the majestic and moving poem called, "The Song of Cadwur." In accordance with bardic practice, he wrote nothing down. It was an oral work intended to be performed widely by recitation or as a song with accompaniment on the lyre.

The poem was first performed to musical accompaniment at the castle of Ambrosius Aemilianus, before him and many of the noble families. They were all deeply moved by the words and music and by the way in which the great bard performed it. As time went by, the poem was performed throughout Britannia and Armorica at courts of kings and at other prestigious venues. It gained equal status to the poems in praise of other famed Celtic heroes, both British and Hibernian from days gone by.

When the poem was performed at the castle of Artorius, Kitto, Nessa and Medar were present to hear it. Afterwards, they were summoned to meet Artorius in his hall. Artorius addressed them all, particularly Kitto, "Dear brave and loyal Kitto, the son of a great and famous warrior, you have served this land with great distinction, in our efforts to defeat our enemies, particularly the Saxons. Your skill and courage saved my life at my time of dire need. Your dear father gave his life for mine.

---

[89] This means Irish Gaelic

"You have done much more than anyone could ever have expected of you, and I would now invite you to return to your own peaceful home, to care for your family and if need be to defend it from any threats it might face.

"My most sincere thanks to Nessa and to Medar for their skilled and devoted assistance in breeding and caring for horses, and for the most generous gift of Cedewain to me. It was tragic that the finest horse I have ever ridden was lost in battle but he will be remembered for all time in song and story.

"Go back home now, my dear friends. We shall always remember you with deep gratitude and affection."

After further dialogue with Artorius, Kitto decided to return to Armorica as his permanent home. He had played his part in defending Britannia, and saw his future as part of his family and as a defender of Armorica, if his services should be needed.

Nessa and Medar also elected to go back home. Nessa was distraught at the loss of her brother, whom she had always thought of as indestructible. She also wept for Cedewain the beautiful stallion which she had bred and reared. It seemed so unfair to her that such a fine animal should die in agony on the battlefield. He had already been put to stud in Rheged and Nessa hoped that thereby his fine bloodline would continue in that northern land.

As the three travelled back to Trepunek, partly by sea and partly over land, they pondered how best to break the sad news to their families. There would be no words able to make this task less than utterly distressing.

Their reunion at Trepunek was filled with emotion: delight that they had returned safely and that the families were together again, but deep anguish at the loss of Cadwur. Most deeply affected were his widow, Rhian, and their children, and Teged, his elderly father now a widower. They took some comfort from being told that Cadwur had died a great hero and would always be remembered as such.

Sadly, great battles give rise to glory as well as to grief, often in equal measure, and to both the victor and the vanquished.

The battles fought by Artorius, with the support of brave cavaliers such as Cadwur and Kitto, were not fought in vain, as there followed a long period of peace and prosperity, with the British and the Saxons each keeping to their own parts of the island. Many of the Saxons were migrant farmers and were content to apply themselves and all their energies to agriculture, in the fertile lands in the east of the country.

Armorica too remained a peaceful land. This was aided by the fact that in the year 493 Clovis, the young king of the Franks, converted to Christianity and was baptised by the distinguished and formidable Bishop of Durocortorum. Clovis' baptism followed his marriage to Clothilda, a Frankish lady who was already a Christian. The Franks' ambition was to take those parts of Gaul held by the Visigoths and drive then into Hispania. They also had the ambition of capturing the lands held by the Burgundians. The Franks did not, however, have their sights set on Armorica, as there were other much bigger targets for them.

Nessa and Medar continued breeding horses, but decided to concentrate on draught horses, for which there was always a demand. Nessa could not face the thought that one of her beautiful animals like Cedewain would perish in great pain on a battlefield.

Kitto could not settle to the life of a farmer and became a permanent member of the militia, with special responsibility for training cavalry recruits. The man who had saved the great Artorius in battle had immediate respect from the young warriors of Armorica. Kitto was rarely called upon to participate in active service, but acquitted himself with distinction when required.

The poem in honour of his father was regularly performed in Armorica. It brought great joy to Kitto to hear the poem performed at Condate from the lips of the bard Dwyryd with his deep and resonant voice in the British language. *The Song of Cadwur* made Kitto's heart swell with pleasure mixed with grief, as he contemplated the heroic life of his father and his own part in saving Artorius.

Epilogue

A retired couple, feeling rather bored, were sitting watching television in their room at a hotel in Reykjavik, when they would have liked to be out of doors seeing the sights of Iceland. The weather was, however, exceptionally inclement, with storm-force winds and driving rain. It was late September in 2024.

Steve said to Bronwen in a rather depressed voice, "I wish we had gone to the cottage in Brittany. It would surely have been warmer and drier than here. I expect that Gareth and Lauren are having a really nice time there."

His wife responded in slightly more optimistic tones, "It's only our first day and they say it's usually quite changeable here. It was your idea to offer the cottage to them and to come here instead, hoping to see the Northern Lights. Let's see if we can get an up-to-date weather forecast on this TV."

Bronwen tried various channels and soon found a suitable one. She knew enough of the Icelandic language to understand the forecast, assisted also by the helpful diagrams. Triumphantly she reported, "Things will be better as from tomorrow afternoon. High pressure is building for the rest of the week. My study of Old Norse is coming in useful, as modern Icelandic is based on it."

Steve seemed reassured. "Well, let's hope the forecast is right." He also knew that there were English speaking channels on the TV, and realised that Bronwen wanted to show off her familiarity with Icelandic.

Steve and Bronwen were educated people, and she knew much of the history of Iceland from her degree level studies. They both knew precious little, however, about geology or science in general. They had come to Iceland to see the Northern Lights (a perfectly sensible reason to go there), but it is a country where it is hard, if not impossible, to avoid seeing geology in action. Their guided tours around the island opened their eyes to the amazing sights in the country's barren and volcanic landscape, interspersed with fine rivers and oases of green fields and woods.

As is the case with many tourists, they were shown mountains, waterfalls, active volcanoes and geysers. The first highlight for Bronwen and Steve was a National Park situated near to Reykjavik, Thingvellir. Iceland is a place where two tectonic plates meet: the North American Plate and the Eurasian Plate. It is the only country in the world where two tectonic plates meet above ground level. The two plates can be observed at the amazing Thingvellir National Park, which has UNESCO heritage status. From a political point of view, Iceland is in Europe but geologically the part of Iceland to the west of Thingvellir is on the North American Tectonic Plate and is therefore in purely geological terms part of North America. It can be said that it is possible to walk between two continents at this historic site.

Steve and Bronwen were having an unexpected crash course on geology and on the history of the Earth. Bronwen already knew about this part of Iceland as the location of the historic parliaments of Iceland, but its importance as a geological site was new to her and she and Steve were delighted to learn about it.

After a few days, despite the excitement of the guided tours, there was disappointment that they had not yet seen the Northern Lights.

Then Bronwen saw a report in the daily Icelandic newspaper, which she more or less understood, about a manuscript which had just come to light at the site of a former Benedictine Monastery in Norway. To understand the article fully, she asked for the help of the hotel receptionist, who spoke fluent English. She was told that the document discovered was thought to be the original manuscript of Njal's Saga written in the late thirteenth century. Excitedly, she told Steve about this amazing find. It was known that the extant manuscripts of this Saga were later versions of it. This was a find of historic importance if it turned out that the original had indeed been found.

Steve's face dropped, as he feared that they would be heading to Oslo, where the precious manuscript had been taken for further study. He also thought that his wife would end up spending weeks studying it, making a new translation of the manuscript and going on to write some sort of novel. He remembered the late night writing sessions in the previous year, from which Bronwen would come to bed at an unearthly hour and wake him up. It had also taken over her whole life.

He was relieved when she told him what she was actually minded to do. "My expertise in Norse literature is not sufficient for me to be involved with this manuscript at a technical level. In due course and if it is confirmed to be what they think it is, I will get hold of a copy to read it for my own interest, but I will leave anything else to the experts in Norway and Iceland. I have no wish to write any sort of fictional story based on the characters in the Saga. I think it would be an impossible task anyway, given the goings on in the story."

Steve was very relieved. There was then some more good news for both of them. He was told by the tour guide that the next night would be very clear. The Sun was at solar maximum, the period which produces the best auroras. The guide added that observations had been made of the aurora in recent days in many locations across Scandinavia. There was every chance of making a sighting on the next night.

This proved to be correct and they were blessed with an utterly spectacular view of the Northern Lights at a viewpoint some miles inland from Reykjavik, near a fishing port. It was not just the aurora which they observed there but also other breath-taking phenomena. On the left of their view was a fabulous aurora, with a double swirl of bright green near the horizon and with a dispersed thinner veil of green higher in the sky. To the centre right of their view was orange gas rising into the sky from an active volcano and further to the right there were three plumes of white gas rising from a geothermal power plant. Added to this were clear reflections in a nearby lagoon of the green of the aurora, the orange of the volcano and the white of the geothermal plant. As an added bonus faint stars were just visible outshone by the aurora.

Steve tried to take photos, but neither he nor his camera were up to the task. It did not matter as the stunning sight which they had witnessed was indelibly printed in their memory.

This rounded off a wonderful holiday for them and they flew back to the UK feeling very happy and satisfied. On the plane, Steve said to his wife how pleased he was that their life would be back to normal now that her research and writing careers were over. Back at home they could think about trips abroad.

His wife responded in a rather matter of fact and academic way, "Oh, but they are not. I meant to tell you that before we left I had a long chat with Rachel at Murray Hill Publishers and they want me to do a sequel to the Song of Cadwur. I am sure I could do one set in the sixth century, following the lives of my characters and their descendants. My novel has the makings of the first part of a saga. There is more reliable written history of the sixth century in Britain and Brittany and I have decided to write a sequel. I can work in the life of St David in Wales, a fictional death of 'King Arthur', the Welsh Founding Saints of

Brittany, the mission of St Augustine to Canterbury, the defeat of the Votadini by the Angles from Northumbria, the Anglo-Saxon conquest of much of Britain, the conquest of the whole of Gaul by the Franks and much more."

It was painfully obvious to him from her assertive language and the look in her eye that she had set her mind on this project and there was no point in trying to dissuade her. He tried to look supportive but could not hide his disappointment.

She just said sympathetically, "I know there were late nights last time and that I couldn't help waking you up sometimes. There is room in the study for a folding bed, and if I want to work late, I can always sleep there."

The plane began its descent to Gatwick, and another chapter in the life of Steve and Bronwen would soon begin. Steve's heart was sinking faster than the plane. Any ideas about foreign trips to distant destinations were on hold for at least another year.

The End

Appendix
Background Historical Information

The Migrants is set in one of the most interesting centuries in British and European history, but one which is sadly lacking in contemporary historical records so far as Britain is concerned. Archaeology continues to yield some useful information from the usual sources such as burial sites, pottery and coins: also from Roman temples which seem to have been converted to churches in the Christian era.

This is the century beginning in the year 400 CE, i.e., the fifth century of the Common Era. It was a time of great change and of the migration of peoples across mainland Europe, and into and out of Britain.

Apart from archaeology, such information as we have regarding events in Britain is based on oral tradition, myth or documents written in later centuries by writers with their own agenda reflecting the attitudes of their time. The best efforts of diligent historians have been able to give us only a sketchy and uncertain account of events in Britain in the fifth century.

It was also the age of perhaps the world's most famous hero of folklore and myth, King Arthur. In the story, I have included a character intended to be the historical figure on whom this mythical king was based.

The story is fiction but I have endeavoured to ensure that it respects what is known or generally believed to be factually correct in that period. When I have made reference to historical persons, I have also tried to be as accurate as possible regarding their lives and deeds.

Although our understanding of the history of this period is vague in many respects, some basic facts are known and it is also reasonable to make some educated assumptions as to other matters.

We know that the Roman legions were withdrawn from Britain by about 407 CE, to help defend the Western Roman Empire from invaders. The British were left to fend for themselves in resisting raids by the Picti and the Scoti, from Scotland and the north of Ireland respectively. We know that the Angles, Saxons and Jutes came into Britain and occupied lands in the eastern side of the country and in the south. Our knowledge of the exact circumstances and timing of their arrival in large numbers is vague and uncertain. But they certainly came to Britain and played a major part in its history in that century and ever since.

We do not know whether their migration was achieved or sustained by regular bloody battles or whether it was relatively peaceful during this century, perhaps with skirmishes. It seems that so far archaeologists have not found evidence of major battles. Historians writing in later times talk of a Saxon Revolt against the British rulers, but what exactly might have happened and when is again vague.

The history of the Saxon conquests in the sixth century (beginning 500 CE) and of British (Welsh) saints going to Brittany in that century is rather better understood, but many events in the fifth century sadly have to be left to speculation.

The title of the story is *The Migrants*, because it is accurate to call this century one of migration on a vast scale; the Anglo-Saxons to Britain; Britons to Gaul and Armorica (Brittany); Germanic tribes crossing the Rhine into Roman Gaul; the Huns invading the lands of the Goths; the Goths in turn driven into the Roman Empire, along with the Vandals; the Vandals invading Spain and being driven out by the Goths; the Vandals then settling in North Africa. In that century, the City of Rome itself was sacked by the Goths and later by the Vandals. Germanic soldiers became Kings of Italy. By the end of the fifth century, the Ostrogoths under their King Theodoric the Great had taken control of Rome and Italy.

Prior to that conquest, the Visigoths were in control of much of southern Gaul and then also of Spain, and the Franks, having migrated into the Roman Empire, became rulers of northern Gaul. The eastern parts of Gaul were under Burgundian control.

Brittany seems generally to have avoided migration other than that of Britons fleeing from their country mainly to escape the Anglo-Saxons. Brittany was a Celtic-speaking enclave in the near continent, which seems already to have had a long connection with Cornwall and with Wales. It seems that it was less troubled by war and conflict than other parts of the continent.

Much of British history is written from an English viewpoint, which is understandable, but, in regard to the fifth century, it has to be written from a British (i.e., Welsh/Celtic) perspective, if for no other reason that England had not yet come into being, whereas Celtic Britain had existed through the Roman occupation and for centuries before that.

The British language was a Brythonic language, a P-Celtic language, from which Welsh, Cornish and Breton evolved. Many Britons would also have known Latin, as the tongue spoken by their occupying power.

When my story begins, the Britons had been living in the Roman province of Britannia for about four hundred years *(about as long as the time from the reign of James the First of England to the present time)*. By then all British freemen were Roman citizens and many would have spoken Latin, as the international language and that of the Church. It is fair to assume that the better-off Britons, and maybe others, were able to read and write Latin, so as to enable them to study the Bible and to understand and respect Roman laws and edicts.

In the fifth century, Britain was a Christian country with a number of bishops. Although some elements of paganism may have persisted and there may have been some doctrinal differences with Rome, its only authorised religion was Christianity. In 313 CE, the Emperor Constantine had legalised Christianity throughout the Empire and in 393 CE the Emperor Theodosius made it the official religion of the Empire, effectively banning other religions. Christianity had already existed in Britain for many years before that, perhaps as early as the second century CE. In the fifth century, there were British bishops and churches, as well as British missionaries, such as St Patrick, who went to Ireland, and St Briog, who went to Brittany.

In my story, the main British characters are literate in Latin and in Brythonic, and committed Christians. I have also made the assumption that there was fervent belief in the Christian Faith during this century, including a belief in miracles, the veneration of saints and a second coming.

The Anglo-Saxon migrants were not at this time either Christian or literate, perhaps with a few exceptions. Their conversion did not even begin until 596 CE when Pope Gregory the Great sent a mission of monks headed by Augustine to Kent to convert its king to the Faith. St David had already been in charge of a bishopric in Wales during that century and Roman Britain had been Christian for over two hundred years. This is not always recognised in the Anglo-centric version of fifth century history.

As for the Franks, who eventually became the major power in Gaul and gave their name to *France*, there had been Christians and bishops among them for many years before their young king, Clovis, was converted in 493 CE.

And so in the century in which the story is set, we find Britons who are Romanised, literate and Christian, unlike the Anglo-Saxon migrants who lacked any of these characteristics.

I have assumed for the sake of the story that some of the wealthier Britons, who had been displaced or threatened with eviction, migrated to Brittany, a Celtic and Christian region, where they could feel at home and away from the threat of attack by the Anglo-Saxons, the Picts or the Scoti.

It seems that the Britons referred to the Angles, Saxons and Jutes simply as the *Saxons*. This view is consistent with the Welsh word for 'English' which is *Saesneg* and the Scots word for it *Sassenach*. I have followed this concept in the story and normally used the word *Saxon* for all the Germanic invaders of Britain.

As regards travel by migrants or by merchants, in ancient times the sea was not always seen as a barrier, as for example the English Channel is in modern times, but could act as a highway. Travel by sea could be faster and safer than over land. A ship could carry a heavier payload than a wagon. Migration and raids were also often carried out by sea-borne invaders. Even as far back as the Phoenicians, long distance sea travel by merchants took place. This is reflected in the story, in which there are several long sea voyages.

I have assumed that there was an historical character on whom the mythical King Arthur was based. If there was such a person, no one knows where he came from, although there are many theories. I have placed him as connected to the Votadini, a Celtic tribe based in the area south of Edinburgh. In that area, we find 'Arthur's Seat'.

I have also assumed that the reported Battle of Badon Hill did take place. If there was such a battle, we do not know for sure the location of Badon Hill or the date of the battle. For the sake of the story, I have assumed that this battle took place in the north of Britain, with the historical warrior on whom King Arthur is based playing a main part in it. I have placed it in 490 CE, to suit the ages of my characters in the story. Some opinion suggests that it occurred about ten years later. As we know little of this battle and as the tale is fictional, I have allowed myself some licence over its date.

To give the story a flavour of its times, I have used the Latin names for towns, cities, countries and regions. Although we are in post-Roman times, the influence of Rome was everywhere, partly from its legacy as an imperial power but also through the Roman Catholic Church and the monastic movement. Latin remained the lingua franca for many more centuries to come.

Although sound historical information for this period is scant, I have tried in my fictional story to avoid anything which is contrary to any known facts or which is anachronistic. If I have in any way erred in these objectives, I hope that this might at least provoke discussion and increase interest in and the study of this shadowy but fascinating period, which was a time of enormous change, paving the way for the development of much of Europe (including the British Isles) in later centuries.

Historical Sources and Background Reading

Constantius of Lyon	Life of Germanus (c480)
St Gildas	De Excidio Britanniae (c 520)
Aneirin	Gododdin—a poem (c 600)
The Venerable Bede	A History of the English Church and People (731/2)
Nennius	Historia Brittonum (c800)
Edward Gibbon	The Decline and Fall of the Roman Empire
Henry Chadwick	The Pelican History of the Church Vol 1 The Early Church
John Morris	The Age of Arthur: A History of the British Isles from 350 to 650
Fitzroy Maclean	A Concise History of Scotland
John Wacher	Roman Britain
Keith Branigan	Roman Britain
David Mattingly	An Imperial Possession: Britain in the Roman Empire (Penguin Part I of History of Britain)
Wikipedia	Numerous entries
History Files Website	Numerous entries